THE HITMAN'S LOVE CONTRACT

RACHEL DOVE

ISBN: 978-1-963705-40-9

Published in the United States of America by Harbor Lane Books, LLC.

www.harborlanebooks.com

Every man is surrounded by a neighborhood of voluntary spies.

JANE AUSTEN

For Lyndsey Maddison
*Who makes the world a brighter, better place every
single day.*

CHAPTER
ONE
BELLA

*Book Title Idea: The Abandoned Housewife Who
Disappeared
Buy milk, pancake mix
Call agent back – beg for more time
Night cream
Botox?*

It was an average Tuesday when Bella finally understood the truth. She hated a lot of her life these days. The realization hit her like a thunderbolt. She could almost see it happen, like an out of body experience as she stood holding on to the shopping cart, knuckles white with tension. A flash of stunning, painful enlightenment, as though a bolt of pure God-like electricity had crashed through the roof of Walmart, striking her body and pinning her to the metal cart, fusing her to it. Singing her skin as it passed through her tired nerve endings and tunneled into the stark cart-marked floor beneath her feet. Sparks hitting the ground through the little rubber wheels, leaving her a burnt little husk. She could almost see it play out as she stood there on that mundane day. How the shoppers around her would react. People speeding off in terror, every direction filled with the chaotic screams of shoppers as they ran away from the tragic woman she'd become.

Hmm, maybe I should write a children's book. One of those parodies for adults. The sad old cow who exploded in the market.

Maybe it was the menopause finally coming to claim her, this melancholy she was feeling. It would explain why she suddenly felt like she was boiling from the inside. Or, perhaps, it was the judgy witch who had just stepped in front of her and decided to ruin her already crappy day.

"Bella, are you okay?" Chrissie was looking at her as if she'd grown an extra head. Christine 'Call me Chrissie' Phelps, possibly *the* worst person to witness her mid-life crisis in the entire Baltimore area they lived in. She was the Queen of the school PTA, part of the Andersen Falls town committee, and the wife of Phillip Phelps, who was part of the town council. All of which meant she spent a lot of her time sitting high on many pedestals and looking down at the little folk. If Mean Girls ever needed an adult recast, Regina's role would be covered by the specimen of passive aggressive woman standing before her. "You look like you just saw a ghost."

I did see a ghost. Mine. I just died during this tedious conversation, and now you're taunting my rather bored corpse. That's what she wanted to say. Instead, she said, "No, I'm fine. Sorry. What was it you were saying?"

Chrissie smiled, showing perfect white teeth behind those perma-glossed red lips. "I was just saying that you're doing so..." She made a point of looking her up and down before she continued. "Well." She pointed a talon her way. Bella's teeth tingled with the sudden urge to bite it off. "You know, considering."

Bella looked down at her oversized sweatpants, belatedly realizing she'd not noticed the maple syrup fingerprints her youngest had left on the right leg. She resisted the urge to pull the hood of her 'Bite Me' hoodie over her head and pull the drawstrings tight enough to garotte herself. She straightened her shoulders instead.

"Yes, well, I'd better get on. Things to do, you know."

"Yes." Christine shuffled on her heels, peering into Bella's trolley like she was a customs official. Her eyes roved over the groceries, and Bella just knew she'd clocked the bottle of wine, potato chips, and rocky road ice cream amongst the Hamburger Helper and other stuff for the kids. "Having a party?"

"Nope," Bella retorted. "What are you doing this morning, Chrissie? Walmart hired cart inspectors now?"

Christine's left eyelid twitched, giving Bella a tiny thrill of petty justice. Her eye always twitched when someone challenged her, which wasn't often enough. She'd first noticed it at one of the meetings at the school last year, when the Halloween decorations hadn't arrived in time for the event she'd been banging on about since the summer. Ever since then, she'd bore it in mind. Used it to push back when she needed to. Like now, for instance, when she was being accosted while getting the groceries in her sweats. She knew she should have shopped online, but she'd been out of coffee. And coconut creamer. She couldn't work without caffeine. She'd need a full pot just to get over this encounter. Possibly with a Valium chaser.

This is why you don't go out, Bella. People. This whole stupid town knows your business, and some of them just love to shove it right in your face. The one standing in front of her was a prime example.

Chrissie was openly staring at her now, and she braced for impact. It felt like that was all she did nowadays. Braced for the onslaught of life, instead of living it. A couple of years ago, she would have been in this supermarket, happy, and getting on with her errands. Eager to get back to the laptop and write whatever new scene was buzzing around in her head. Now? She was an empty shell, devoid of passion, of fight. Of anything that made her *her.* She wouldn't have sweated Chrissie, she'd have even laughed about the interaction. Used it as fiction fodder. Brace, brace, brace. Brace and wait for the old her to come back.

If this was a scene from one of her books, she might have had her character retreat with a clever retort or a cutting reply, but alas. She didn't have it in her anymore. Couldn't remember a time she had it, come to think of it. She was tired of fighting, tired of putting on a damn brave face for everyone and her kids, who had been through the ringer the last few months and were looking to her to pull them through it. She was the fish in the round glass bowl, with no fake castle to hide in. This was real-life, small-town mentality.

Not gonna happen.

No matter how angry she felt, gripping the cart for dear life as if it was some tether to the earth, she'd definitely make the jungle drums rumble if she stoved the PTA Queen's stupid face into the canned goods aisle. So, she did what she had been doing for as long as she could remember. She stood there smiling and took the shit.

"It's good that you kept your sense of humor." Christine's grin was feline, half feral. "Despite what your ex-husband says, you're actually quite funny."

"Aww, thanks, honey." Bella drew a slow breath in,

making sure her smile was about as far away from her eyes as she could get it. Bringing Gerry into this was below the belt, and they both knew it. Chrissie's narrowed piggy eyes told her she'd made her point, despite Bella's attempts at faux civility in the face of her straight-up bitchery. "Was there something else you wanted? I have things to do, deadlines to meet."

"Of course." Prissy Chrissie beamed. Her face must have hurt, exerting all that fakeness onto her bronzed jaw line. "I'll let you get on. Double the work, eh? Being on your own," she simpered. "No wonder you look so tired. And…" Her eyes roved up and down once more, and Bella resisted the sudden urge she felt to flip her off. "Well, the casual look is favored by the single moms, I guess. Hides those extra pounds quite nicely." She looked down at herself. "Or, so I hear." She flashed another toothy fake grin to really bring the burn home. "Don't forget the PTA meeting after school next Thursday, okay?"

She swished past with her little smug basket, a cloud of expensive perfume choking Bella in her wake.

"Bitch," Bella muttered under her breath.

Thursday was going to be hellish. She hadn't forgotten about the damn meeting. That would be impossible unless she lived under a rock or entered witness protection. The PTA were the worst at the phone tree shizzle. This week alone she'd had 14 emails and 4 texts reminding her of the meeting date and time, while also pushing agenda items that quite literally were the point of the meeting in the first place.

The other mothers were busy, too. Who wasn't a modern mother and not juggling five things in an average minute? Sometimes, she felt like it was just some kind of secret race that no one had told her about, and one she was permanently losing. Wasn't it enough that she kept her spawn alive and fed? Happy? The PTA meeting was like a gauntlet of Pinterest-scented failure.

Eyeing the wine in her basket, wishing she had given in and bought two, she pushed it to the back of her mind. She didn't have long till school pick-up, and she still had to go to the gas station, the dry cleaners, and make a phone call she couldn't put off any longer. Heading down the cereal aisle, she grabbed Poppy's favorite and rechecked the list she'd scribbled down that morning. She'd just about got everything she needed. As she headed to the checkout, she noticed people looking in her direction. With a deep, bone shaking sigh, she pulled up the hood of her sweatshirt and focused on getting home without going viral. Again.

———

Standing at the gas station pump, her mind wandered. *What the fucking fuck am I going to do with my life?*

This was the eternal question. Life was one long gauntlet of exhaustion and panic, all swimming in a sea of shame and straight up embarrassment. It was akin to being tortured, having a slow but certain nervous breakdown whilst trying to keep the wheels on at home. She was on autopilot half the time, present but vacant when the kids were at school or out with their friends. It was all so dull, with no relief in sight.

When did she become this woman? Where was the girl who had dreams and wishes of her own? Had she really let life and *him* melt them away? And now that there was no one to share this life with, what was left? Was this it, till the children grew up and left her alone? It felt like a cruel joke, watching the woman she used to be disappear under the monotony of being left, literally holding the babies. No wonder the birth rates were dropping. The illusion that being a breeder was the epitome of life was fading in favor of financial security, freedom, and not being well and truly dicked over by the man you had pledged your life to over a decade ago. Leaving her to this, hiding in the grocery store from beady-eyed busy bodies who thought they knew her just because of some salacious headlines.

So, here she was, deep in the day to day. The monotony of spending time making dinner every night, especially for kids who declared any vegetable to be gross and would prefer pizza rolls, anyway. All while trying to keep hold of a career that felt like it was more than happy to leave her behind.

Bella sometimes wished she'd actually trained to do something productive other than pursuing English. She'd flirted with the law once upon a time. Maybe if she hadn't listened to her creative notions, she would be a lawyer now. Financially stable, and maybe even able to actually do something about the hell she'd found herself living lately. Instead of sitting in front of a desk at home, pretending to write for hours and hours, whilst secretly watching true crime shows on Netflix and googling *Henry Cavill + shirtless + growly*.

And looking at various dating sites her agent sent her, and then not signing up. She'd filled in the profiles a handful of times, but when she hit preview on the finished profile, that's when the instinct to bail overruled everything else. It all looked so sad and pathetic up there on the screen, her dull life in black and white, the space for the profile picture blank and mocking. She barely had any recent photos, full stop. She was normally behind the camera, or in the background. The selfies she'd tried to take recently looked like the before shot for a therapy advert. She'd deleted the lot. The only thing she was grateful for body wise lately was the fact that the stress and upheaval had shifted a few pounds, but given that she hid her pre-child body weight in baggy clothes, anyway, it was a hollow comfort at best. Although, given Chrissie's barb earlier, the loose clothes were doing a fine job at maintaining the dowdy pudgy façade she had subconsciously been cultivating.

If she had the energy to go through her wardrobe, she could probably find her old stuff. The lush vintage jeans she loved too much to throw away, for one thing. But that meant going into her closet and seeing the empty side of the rail. Last time she'd delved in there for something to wear for a book event, she'd found an old shirt of Gerry's, and that had led to a whole half hour of rage with a pair of fabric scissors, followed by three tequilas and an early night as soon as the kids crashed. So, she'd stuck with the sweats. Which didn't exactly scream 'date me'.

She had photos, of course. Loads with the kids. Theme parks, zoos, petting farms. Cinema trip selfies, and shots the kids had taken of her, all giving her five chins and five o'clock shadow with the most unflattering angles. But still, she was there. There was documented evidence that she had been there for their lives. She was usually the one behind the lens, threatening her kids with no ice cream if they didn't smile in unison for the perfect hashtag blessed, hashtag family day out shizzle she was planning to put on Instagram later. She had photos, just nothing she would want to put out for the world to see. Her photo albums went from her being a lithe, fresh faced twenty something, draped across various friends and the occasional hot love interest to…well, none. Those photos were amazing, but they were too outdated. Catfish territory. Plus, she didn't look or feel one iota like she did when she was the person in those photos.

Now, after recent events, she had even less of a clue just what her purpose on the planet was, other than writing total garbage she felt sure no one would ever read again and cleaning the pee off the toilet seats at home four times a day. This identity crisis wasn't exactly the greatest thing to kick off a dating profile with. She could imagine her profile description now:

Former carefree, late thirty-something seeks honest man to share current banal existence with. Must like children. Needs to have lived under a rock with no wi-fi for the last six months. Cheaters definitely need not apply.

No, that would be too obvious.

One woman man? Well, that should be obvious, shouldn't it? She'd thought so, when she'd first started her deep dive into the murky world of researching online dating, but she'd already seen two men on there that she knew for damn sure were married in real life. Lonely hearts, it seemed, were not the only organs searching for a little something something. Which made her lady parts want to shrivel up and die off.

She was just pulling the nozzle out when a sleek black car pulled up behind her minivan. As she turned to look, the back door opened and out stepped the most beautiful man she'd ever seen. No word of a lie, he was straight off one of the covers of her favorite romance novels. So hot he didn't look real, standing there at the local gas station of her sleepy little town. And, of course, she met his eye by accident.

Seriously? She mumbled under her breath, trying and failing to look away. *I look like a street rat and Abercrombie and Fitch just pulled up.* Blushing, she yanked her eyes off him, but not before he'd locked his with hers. Which meant he was probably a half second away from dismissing her as some kind of weird gas pumping troll. She didn't need the rejection of a stranger to add to her already lower than a snake's belly self-esteem. Shrugging her head further back into her hood, she pretended to concentrate on the screen in front of her whilst getting a good look at the guy.

Mr. Not-From-Around-Here looked like he'd just driven off Wall Street. His suit was probably worth more than her van, his shoes black and shiny like the car he'd driven in. He was h-o-t. Hot. Tall, dark, handsome. He had one of those faces that was symmetrically perfect, but also so perfect you couldn't have picked him out of a line-up.

"Hey."

Shit. The male model was looking in her direction. Turtling back into her hood, she whirled around to see who he was talking to. Presumably some supermodel who was also in the Falls to get random Tuesday afternoon gas. The lot was empty except for them. *Weird.*

"Sorry, I didn't mean to startle you."

She peeked back his way, and he was standing two feet away. His smile was like looking into the damn sun. It was so warm and delicious she could feel the heat. Hell, it had probably melted the syrup globules on her sweatpants. *Oh God, syrupy sweatpants.*

"Switfokay."

Dear God.

"It's okay," she tried again, feeling her top lip stick to her teeth. She covered her mouth to hide it.

"I was just saying hello," he said patiently, as if adult conversation was normal for him. Which, of course, it was. For him and most of the human race. Especially the ones who hadn't been outed as the unknowing spouse all over the internet. Mr Gas Station hottie wouldn't know anxiety if it hit him in the face, she was guessing. He didn't exactly look the type to get tongue tied and flustered. This hunk could quite possibly call the birds from the trees with a flick of a wrist like a Disney prince. *Unlike me, who currently feels like a bridge troll.*

"Right," she said dumbly.

His lips twitched, and she wanted to fucking die. With a nod of his head, he turned to the pump. "So, hello. Have a good day."

"Er, yeah. You too." He didn't take his eyes off her, pulling out the pump and driving it home with an ease that made Bella think of about twenty different and far dirtier names for a nozzle in her head. She missed putting hers back, fumbling fingers missing the hole several times before she managed to finally lock it back into place. Fumbling for the receipt, she half dove into her seat. In her rearview mirror, she was pretty sure he was chuckling to himself as he watched her drive away.

"Girl," she said to the tired woman staring back at her in horror, "you have to get your shit together. That was embarrassing."

Bella took a deep glug of the lukewarm cup of coffee on her desk, pulling a face but then draining the cup, anyway. Caffeine was caffeine, and after the dawn raid that morning by her kids, the snarking incident in Walmart, and the very unsettling yet steamy gas nozzle debacle, she was in need of all the legal stimulants she could cram into her very tired and frazzled body.

The incident at the gas station had confirmed something for her. A couple of things, actually. One was that she could still appreciate a damn fine looking man, despite her lack of libido in recent months. But that was a moot point, because the second thing she'd learned was that looking for a man was pointless. Even if she could meet someone half decent, and get the energy to actually boff him, the chances were it would be doomed. With everything she had going on, it would take a strong man to come into her goldfish bowl of a life and keep up with the kids.

She was old and jaded enough to know that such a man didn't exist. Not in real life. She could probably find plenty in the pages of her favorite books, but a flesh and bone member of the opposite sex? Not. A. Chance. And even if one did fancy life with a single mom, why the hell would he want her? The man would have to thrive on chaos, mixed in with mundanity. The type of guy she wanted did exist, but sadly, only in the stories she and her fellow authors invented in their books. Gas station guy was a perfect example. She was pretty sure he was some kind of gasoline fueled mirage. In fact, she was half tempted to ask Gas Station Gus if she could check his CCTV footage just to be sure.

The dating site was mocking her from the laptop. The images of nauseatingly happy and loved up couples taunted her, as if they had her dream man ready and waiting like some Ken doll in a box. All shiny and new and ready to live life to the fullest and go rollerblading on the beach. It was a shame, really, that she couldn't just order a man like she could order take-out. Maybe she could, but probably not the kind who could share pancakes with her kids on a Sunday morning.

Not that Gerry did that often when they were together.

Sighing, she clicked off the Internet screen and returned to the novel she was supposed to be writing, as per the advance she'd already spent. The blank page glared back at her. Her agent was going to be calling any minute for an update, and she had nothing. No dating profile set up, and no book. No story. Nada. Zip. Not a sausage. Literally.

She was supposed to be well on with her latest steamy romance book, but her idea well was as dry as the Saraha sand. Perhaps, if she wrote thrillers for a living, it would have been easier to navigate the changes her life had undergone recently, but she wrote about everlasting love. People who ripped each other's clothes off and couldn't breathe without the other person near them. Characters who admired their love interests from afar. Burned the world down, obsessed with the beating heart of the other. When one of her fictional characters was given the chance of love, or even just making their chosen paramour's life easier, they did everything. Anything. George O'Malley throw-themselves-in front-of-a-bus anything.

Which was much easier to construct on the page when she was one of the sad saps herself. Now, she wished her ex-husband would kindly stop breathing or shuffle off to some other planet. She was chronically and very publicly single, and her fans were already messaging her asking about the next book release. Which was scheduled to be on…well, the twelfth of never, unless she managed to pull her finger out and actually write it. She already knew that Jennifer, her longstanding and currently long-suffering agent, had scheduled the phone meeting to discuss just that. Her emails had been getting more frantic with every ping into her inbox. She wanted to discuss covers, title ideas, and marketing strategies. None of which could be done without the damn product.

She needed a bestseller more than ever. Her last book hadn't quite been the success she was used to. If this next one flopped, the advances would probably be smaller, harder to get. Her last one had done okay, but not the usual Carmicheal sales record. She'd written it in the early days of her life crisis, and it was fuelled by tears and rage in the small hours when the kids were in bed. She was proud of it, but it had been a departure from her usual upbeat novels. It was a book woven from her anger and pain. It had broken the mold of her others, and not in a good way, apparently. It had gained her new readers but served to alienate some of her devoted ones.

If she believed the reviews.

Which she did, especially when devouring them one after the other at three in the morning while eating the raw cookie dough she'd hidden from the kids. The online jury had read between the lines and delivered their verdict. The romance had died off for Bella Carmichael, and her book about a divorcee finding her way in the world through friendship and inner discoveries hadn't quite hit the mark for her core fan base. The readers were all saying the same thing: Bella's next book was one to wait for. And she could feel their bated breath on the nape of her neck every time she sat in front of her keyboard.

After another ten minutes of staring at the blinking cursor, she sighed and dragged herself off to her secret cupboard. Maybe another hit of cookie dough would kickstart the gray matter.

CHAPTER
TWO
JOHN

Rule One: No witnesses.
Rule Two: No evidence.
Rule Three: No connections.

The dark figure skimmed the wall with his back, keeping his eyes focused. All of the possible entry and exit points were just as they should be, his recon impeccable as usual. He didn't want to be here, but it would be the best opportunity before the CEO of the firm headed back to Brazil and made getting the job done much harder. Not impossible, of course, but it would involve more risk, and that wasn't something he either welcomed or took for granted. It had to be today, right here, where any number of the CEO's enemies could be blamed in the aftermath.

Not that it mattered who they thought was to blame, because it would never come back on him. These fuckers would never know who had hit them. Besides, he wanted to get paid from the job and move the hell on. He'd already told

Hannah that he wouldn't be doing any overtime. Enough was enough. He wanted to head back to the States, and then he was O-U-T out. Back to his own plan for once. He knew just the place he'd visit first, too.

The building was right on the waterfront, a nondescript looking structure that looked like every other one alongside it to the untrained and deadly eye. But it had one major difference. If you walked into this one uninvited, you would soon know about it. Security was everywhere, ever watchful.

The back of the building backed on to the rocks, right along the choppy water's edge. The boulders below were craggy, sharp, and battered by the raging waves.

He walked along, back flush to the wall, as close to the stone as he could get without scraping his skin off. Above, the security camera looked right above him. Their all-seeing eye, watching the water for invaders from the ocean. He was unseen from their angle, and the darkness of the night matched him. All that could be seen through his get-up were his eyes, and the waters he'd emerged from shone inky black. No reflection, no sapphire blue. It looked like oil, slick and thick and the color of midnight. No one expected an attack from there. It was suicide. He'd banged his shin on the way up the rocks, but he barely felt the pain with the cold seeping through his wetsuit.

He reached for his belt and opened his waterproof bag. He knew by his watch he had seconds to get into position. Pulling out his weapon, a 9mm Glock with a silencer attached, he checked it over. As he was zipping the bag, his phone lit up. It was a secure line, so he didn't have to worry about any cellphone towers. He was about to ignore it, but something on the screen gave him pause. The next job. The last one. Right back where he wanted to be. Hannah had sent the brief. Good. One step closer.

Hiding the lit-up screen, he returned to scanning the ramparts of the building. He could see the noses of the security guards every time they looked over periodically, but his position was hidden.

Moving on silent, surefooted feet along the rocks, his neoprene shoes gripped the surface as he steeled himself for the moment. He raised his gun high above his head, zeroing in on a spot just over the wall above him. He couldn't hear much over the sound of the ocean, but he could see the telltale wisp of cigarette smoke of the CEO's right-hand man, Erick. Men and their cigars. The male of the species were nothing without their little rituals. Vices were weaknesses, especially in his line of work. The hard-faced bastard up there was as addicted to the Cuban cigars he constantly puffed on as he was hookers and making people disappear. It was his signature move to stub his butt ends out on the foreheads of his enemies. *Yep, a real sweet guy.*

John's eyes zeroed in on the smoke and waited. Erick was there, looking out to sea, talking in his native tongue into his smartphone. Someone called his name, and he turned, nodding once to the visitor. *Yuri.* This was it. His penultimate job. Next time he went to Brazil, it would be to take in the sights, not take someone out for a change. He waited, his breath steady, until one head became two. The pair of men started speaking, and the pair of them leaned out. Creatures of habit, just like he said.

Holding his breath, he waited. Finger primed on the trigger. One job down, one to go. The second Erick ended the call, he took his shots.

Phut. Phut. Phut.

Erick was hit in the jaw, and he went down like a sack of shit as the bullet tunneled into his brain. Yuri took his in the side of the cheek, the other right through the jugular. As the arterial spray shot out, hitting the water, John tucked himself into the rock to avoid being showered by bits of Yuri's broken facial bones. Erick's cigar fell from his mouth, and as John jumped off the rocks into the sea, diving mask on and gun back in his bag, he heard it sizzle as he hit the water. Extinguished, once and for all.

The sirens and the shouting started moments after. As he rose to draw a breath, he heard the bemused commotion start to reverberate around the building he left behind. As he swam under the surface of the ocean, heading for his hidden boat, he thought of the face he'd seen mere days before. One he'd not been prepared for, while he was out on a far less deadly recon mission. A job that he'd turned down because it was so far out of his remit it was laughable.

He swam around a large jutting rock, the movements of his limbs precisely cutting the water like a hot knife through butter. A fish peeked out from its hiding place to look at him. Even in the infinite dark, the bright blue hue from its scales reflected back from his waterproof torch light. As though the little thing had come to help light his way back. Back to something he'd been looking for for some time. Had wanted before his own mind had even voiced it to his consciousness.

Seeing her that day, so unscripted, utterly uncontrived–it had nearly knocked him off his feet. It commanded his thoughts ever since. As the fish swam away, he had a thought that came unbidden. One he didn't want to discard to reason. He didn't believe in coincidences, fate, any of that. The future was what a man decided for himself by every decision he ever took. She shouldn't have been there that day, breathing the same air as him. Close enough to talk to, to feast on with his eyes. He'd been looking for the next step that came after all...this.

Maybe she was it. The light to his dark.

He never used to be the type of man who believed in all that in real life and not just in the books he devoured in his lonely line of work. The love stories he read in secret when he was alone contained something he never thought of having for himself. Maybe that was what attracted him to reading them in the first place.

There was a huge attraction for book lovers to the morally gray heroes and anti-heroes, he knew, but that couldn't translate to real life. *His life.* It was a choice he made long ago, to stay in the shadows. To never have roots or put something first for himself. It was a decision he'd lately been trying to remind himself that he'd made freely.

The stories from his favorite author had felt like a half decent compromise once upon a time. Like he could live that life vicariously, while he did the dirty work and stayed out of life to do it.

Doing the job he did was hard, but it used to thrill him, too. Changing the world for the better, more than any pontificating politician or affluent philanthropic billionaire. Behind the scenes, he actually shaped history. Righted wrongs. Saved people. He travelled, saw the world. Worked on his own schedule, which kept him sharp and engaged in the meaning behind it all. He was never one for the nine-to-five, after all. Who would be? It was monotonous and boring. Just look at popular culture. If James Bond suddenly quit his job to be a pen salesperson, would people still watch? Nah. They wanted to see him take threats to humanity out *with* pens, not sell them in boxes. They wanted him to put *people* into boxes and be suave doing it. The only difference between those heroes and him was the fact that they got the girl, too.

These were the thoughts that consumed him, even now, as he cut through the dark water like a sharp knife through giving flesh.

As he finally clicked off his light and broke the surface of the water, he felt his muscles burn from the exertion. *This was much easier in my twenties. Hell, I could do two hits in a day and still have the energy to work out after.* The other week, a damn hotel bed had left him with a back so creaky he thought he was being followed.

Hauling himself up into the boat, he remembered the day he'd realized he wanted out, and how the realization had shocked him more than what he'd just done. More than anything he'd ever done. That day in Dubai, he'd made a choice and had told Hannah that this was it. He was executing the exit plan he'd always kept for someday, never truly believing he'd want or need to use it.

The fact was he'd felt envious for a second about the pen sellers of the world. The people who led those mundane lives he protected from the shadows. Perhaps, it really was time to change things up, he'd thought. See how the other half lived. Hannah had tried to talk him out of it, of course. The agency wouldn't like it, but screw them. He'd taken his role with a clause in his contract for just such an occasion. He'd work for them, but when he pulled the ripcord, that was that. Communication was severed, and one never existed to the other. As long as the secrets remained dead in the ground, they were good. No comebacks. They knew he'd be ready for them if they tried to object. The shield they'd trained wouldn't be taken down, not even by them. One last job, and he was free to be whoever he wanted to be.

In the far distance, he could just make out the buildings in the distance. Search lights scanned overhead, but not further than the rocks. They hadn't detected him, just as he'd planned. In and out, before they even realized anything was amiss.

Peeling off his wetsuit and shucking on a pair of jeans, he

tapped out a text on the phone from his bag. A reply pinged back. A half second later, he got the notification from his offshore bank account. The money for the job was in. Mission almost accomplished. Time for retirement, without the gold watch. Only a few loose ends to tie up, and he was off to…wherever he wanted to. To be whoever he wanted to be.

That is, if he could ignore the gnawing feeling deep down in his gut. The one that told him his new life might not be the prize he'd wanted for so long. Since he was a lonely kid in trouble with the law, plucked from obscurity and trained to rid the world of evil from the darkness the shadows afforded him. For the first time in his adult existence, not knowing what would happen next didn't fill him with the same euphoria it once did. Chaos he thrived in, but uncertainty was an unknown quantity. It threatened to make him its bitch, and one thing he had never been was someone else's bitch. The early days at the agency had proved that point to him, and when he got to be the best in his field, he made sure they all knew it, too.

He stowed everything away in the hold, started the ignition, and pulled on a sweater and a baseball cap to avoid any onlookers. To them, he would just look like an angler, a night boater. They wouldn't be able to pick him out of a line-up. Not that he'd even been close to being in one. For a hired killer, he was one of the best. Quick and clean. He'd never even been caught speeding. Not on his own plates, anyway. There was that time in Vienna that got a bit hairy. He'd had to bribe an official that time, but naked photos with the mistress weren't hard to find with most men in power. The more money and status people gained, the further they rose, and the farther away the rules of decency became.

Pulling back the throttle, he eased out of the alcove and

headed for open water. He had at least half an hour before they cottoned on to the water escape and galvanized the troops of shitheads in time. He'd be long gone by then. A whisper of wind on the water.

His phone buzzed when he was a few miles from his destination. Hannah. One thing he wouldn't miss about his handler was her work ethic. He would barely finish one job before she was chasing him to confirm another.

The shoreline came into view, the lights along the ridge showing him he was right on target. His waiting car was a quick ride away from the airport. By tomorrow, he would be back stateside and ready for the next step in his new life. Once he got the job request squared off and rightly denied, Hannah and his vocation would be out of his life and he could finally make a new one.

As he steered the boat toward the dockside, he pulled up the info on his secure phone. His last job request was unusual, and not what he'd reconned. So unusual that the agency didn't even refer them to the handlers, let alone hired guns like him. A domestic undertaking, which he normally didn't do. One, the money wasn't in it, and two–it was usually more than morally gray. He only took jobs that weren't a love rival bumping off another, or some seedy hired hit. He liked to think the people he took out actually caused a ripple of good in the world, not adding another layer to the thick underbelly of society. The human race was pretty good at ripping itself apart without his special set of skills tipping the balance further.

Something was off. It was still in the same place, but the details didn't match up. He scanned the limited information, one eye on the shoreline as he pulled back on the engine. When he saw the name of his next target, he almost lost control. Cursing, he scowled at the details. The irony of it all.

What the hell was going on? When he'd come to a sleek stop, he tied up the boat and speed dialed Hannah.

"So," she purred when he answered, "Last job a go? I know it's not your usual style, but the others are all further afield. Given the deadline you gave me for your *notice*," the sarcastic tone clear in her voice, "I figured I would ask. You asked for the US for your last hoorah. I could put Jennings on it, but you know him."

He was already scowling at the thought of how Jennings would deal with the job. As messy as possible. Collateral damage was considered a whoopsie to that douche canoe.

"Not a fucking chance," he growled. "This job is not for us or anyone else. It's a domestic, kill the job." He was not the silent assassin he'd become over the years because he chose to wade in with his size elevens unprepared and unsure of the job, and whether or not it was the right course of action. He wasn't some hired gun like Cyrus Jennings. "Put the word out, too," he added with a rumble to his tone. "If anyone else moves on this job, I'll take the bastards out myself."

"Thought you might say that," Hannah replied, the smile evident in her voice. "The client won't be dissuaded. I told him we weren't interested initially, but he said if it wasn't us it would be someone else he hired."

"So, you already tried to kill it, before you sent me the job? The way you sent me on that bullshit scoping exercise? Did you know who it was?"

He thought back to the recent recon she'd sent him on. He'd truly believed it was a damn coincidence, being there. Near her. What an idiot.

"Yep. I figured I'd let you figure it out for yourself. Kismet, right? Your last job, and it's this. Why do you think I sent you to Baltimore in the first place?" She had the audacity to laugh. "Seriously, you are slipping. Probably best you hang up your holsters. Buy those Crocs everyone wears."

"You told me to check into a coffee shop owner. One that was ninety if she was a day, and the only thing I found out about her was that her sons were trying to get her to 'retire' so they could sell the place out from under her and get top dollar. Which I already told you, we don't do. I was going to turn the job down and you know it. One more consideration, and I was done. We agreed. You didn't have to send me there on some wild goose chase. I don't like being played, Hannah."

"Did you see her there?" She ignored his tone. "It's a usual haunt of hers, from our intel. The publicity says she's a New Yorker, fake address. I'm guessing that was to make her seem more glam. Her books are pretty racy. So, did you see her?"

"No," he snapped back. *I didn't see her there. Not at the café, anyway. So much for coincidence. I'd put it down to a lucky twist of fate I didn't believe in. Color me unhappy.* "I said I was out, Hannah. After this, I am. It won't be a kill job."

"I knew the second it came in that you were the man for the job."

"Stop gloating," he warned. He heard her tutting reply.

"Have we met?" she quipped. "Listen, it's not our usual, sure, but the client will get this done one way or another. Since you are leaving, anyway, I figured one blot on your perfect record won't mean much, and I have no knowledge. Or trail." She'd already covered her tracks. Hannah was annoying, like a little sister, but she was good. She knew him better than he thought, too. Had paid more attention to his private life, such as it was. She was right, though; he wouldn't want this job to go anywhere else. Wouldn't allow it. "It was pretty amazing that it fell into our lap first. I think it's kismet, you know? Her biggest fan getting hired? You can't write that shit."

"She probably could," John replied, his mouth running away with him before he could stop it.

And she could write it. The woman was a wordsmith. Her books were racy, sure. But not just that, they were well thought out in their characters, the settings, and the plots were always unique in each and every story she put out there. Taking that from the world? Erasing her? Not a chance.

Hannah, oblivious to his inner thoughts, continued. "She has kids, too, so it's important that we get this right. No innocents."

"Yeah, well, the client doesn't seem to be bothered about the blowback, does he?"

"Read his file, John. He's not exactly a moral standing kind of guy."

Oh, I'll be reading his file. I'm going to find out every detail.

"My point is, you can't have this big retirement and not have your favorite author to turn to."

"You make it sound like I'm just going to buy lounge pants, read books, and crochet."

"Aren't you?"

He pinched his lips tight. Damn Hannah. She always knew the right thing to say to get her way. It was true, he was looking forward to a quiet life. His favorite author being bumped off would be annoying. Especially since he'd planned to visit her as soon as he was free. This, well…it escalated things, to say the least. "Look, if you don't take the job, someone else will. I like her books, too. I don't think this is right, John. Consider this a parting gift, one colleague to another."

"Jasper won't like it. You know how this will go down." The leader of the agency was already annoyed to lose his biggest money earner. Deliberately messing up jobs would not go down well at all.

Hannah snorted. "Well, your exit papers are signed, either way. When it landed on my desk, what could I say? I figured it was fate."

"I don't believe in fate."

"I know," she sighed. He could hear the rush of air come through the line so clear he could almost feel it caress his ear. "But this job, coming through right when you're about to hang up your holsters? I don't know. Maybe fate believes in you."

His sigh was saturated with exasperation. "Or a sign I should have handed in my papers earlier."

"Whatever," Hannah huffed. "This landed into your lap for a reason, Mr. Black. Take the job or find some other way to fill your days as a man of leisure. You will have to find a new favorite author, though. Maybe you could join a book club." He heard the tapping of keys at the other end of the phone. "I can deal with Jasper. Not everything's about money, Black."

"Tell Jasper that when you break the news."

"Oh, I will. Just get on it, before the hit gets taken out of our hands. Check it out, see how serious the client really is. It could be nothing."

"Sure." Ordering a hit on a person in your life wasn't something people did on a whim. In his experience, once the money was agreed and the deposit sent, it was as good as done. Hiring the agency wasn't like pinning an all-expenses-paid trip to some wish list on Google. The threat was real enough. Now, he just had to decide what he was going to do about it. "I'll be there tomorrow. See how the land lies."

"Good. Tickets are already booked. I am sending you the info for your identity through the secure network. Safe flight, Black. The locker will be ready."

He grunted a reply, eager to get off the phone and be out of there. He was so pumped up he couldn't think straight.

What are the fucking chances, he thought, before snapping the handset in half and throwing the phone into the sea. And now, he had to wait to get to the airport to start his surveillance and make sure he didn't have any interference. The lack of technology in his possession was another reason to change things up. He was pretty sure pen sellers and office workers didn't need a new phone more often than they changed their socks. Having a base that wasn't some soulless, out of the way bolt hole wouldn't be half bad, either, if only so he could actually have some stuff to keep in it for once.

One more job, he told himself as he slid into the black leather seat of his rental. Something told him that this one would be one to remember. It was time to get started. His pretty prey was waiting.

CHAPTER
THREE
BELLA

"Just a second, honey. Mom's on the phone."

She gave her kids the best loving smile she could, before pulling the pantry door closed behind her and releasing the rage bubbling up inside. That familiar gut roil that punched her in the stomach.

"You really are a fucking prick, you know that? I can't believe I ever touched you. I must have been deranged."

"Oh, come on, you know you loved it." He was using the smarmy, cooing voice she'd always hated. At one time, in the early days, she'd fallen for it so many times. Convinced he was being sincere and not condescending. It made her teeth grind. She huffed as he chuckled, feeling the fury rise to new levels as she gripped the phone tight to her ear.

"Loved it? Hardly. Who could love that when it was over before it began half the time? Now, listen, you limp dicked, whisky cocked asshole, I am not–repeat not–selling this house. I fucking paid for half of it, and I'm paying for it now!"

"Oh, really? How come I got this bill, then?"

"Oh, I get it." She peeped out of the doorway, checking

that her kids weren't listening at the other side. She could hear shouts of 'gerroff' and the noise of Breakfast Television, which meant she had about three minutes before all hell broke loose. "That's why you suddenly called, is it? The money. Of course. Why should I ask for you to provide for your kids when you would rather stick it up your nose or spend it on that zygote you call a girlfriend? The children are fine by the way, other than being late for school because their useless father rang to pick a fight."

"Oh, that's perfect, B. Kiss our kids with that mouth?"

"Listen, I know where *your* mouth has been in graphic detail, so you can just fuck off trying to imply parental guilt. You hardly see your kids, and when you do, your staff end up babysitting while you're God knows where doing God knows what! Don't call me B, either. You lost that right when you stuck your dick in everything with a damn pulse. It's Bella to you, and next time you want to ring me when I need to do the school run to moan about how hard your life is, stick it up your tight little pucker and go through my solicitor. Kapesh?"

She cut the call off as he was just drawing breath through his stupid, pudgy cheeks to fire something else back at her. After allowing herself a whole twenty seconds to sag against the shelves and try to quell her inner frustration, she fired off an email to her solicitor, asking him to give her a call to discuss the game plan. It would cost her, but every day with him had cost her. At least in their current state of affairs, the hit might only be financial.

Selling the house was not an option. She had worked just as much as he had in those early days, helping to set up his first dealership. She'd decorated the whole house herself, made sure the house ran smoothly. Raised the kids while he spent all day every day building up his empire. Carmichael Gyms, Carmichael Cars. The guy was never happy with just one thing, and that should have been a big red flag from the off. He had all the money, held all the cards, because whilst she helped him build the portfolio, her name wasn't on it. He wouldn't even have half of what he did if she hadn't been there to support him. Now that she had finally got rid of him, he was trying to get out of paying his fair share.

Selling the house was a cheap move. It wasn't like he wanted it or needed the money. No, as usual, he just wanted to save a buck, and since the house was worth ten times what they paid, she would burn it to the ground before she saw a For Sale sign out front. This was their home, her and the kids, and he wasn't going to take it away because he didn't want to pay for the family he had helped build. And destroy.

CHAPTER
FOUR
GERALD

"Bitch! What a fucking bitch!"

The horn honked in short bursts, his fists hammering on the steering wheel. His cell was thrown hard onto the passenger seat, his finger stabbing down on the power button.

The radio clicked on, providing the soundtrack for him squealing off his drive. Well, his mother's driveway. Because his wife had his house, didn't she? Leaving him to live in his mother's shitty bungalow. He couldn't put money down on a new place because the settlement wasn't sorted and he needed to keep things cheap. So, here he was, living in his mother's frilly chintz décor. Rent free, sure, but not for long, since the old coot had gone into a nursing home and now his sister was selling up to pay for her care. Well, Tracy had always been a bit of a selfish cow. Didn't she realize that would make him homeless? It's not as if his mother needed it, was it? She already had room and board.

He was getting desperate, too. They had five viewings that evening. Tracy had stripped the place out, taking stuff for her mother and arranging for the rest to be sold. And he wasn't going to get anything out of it, so it wasn't like he had any cash coming his way. He had suggested that perhaps Tracy should just move their mother in with her, or find her somewhere a bit cheaper, but Tracy was having none of it. Sure, she had the kids to look after, and Mom was a bit on the senile side, but she was being a total drama queen. Mom had only walked down the street naked a couple of times, and the fire in the garage wasn't that bad. It's not like it reached the house.

The people around him were just so self-centered. Never thinking about Gerald and his needs and wants. Everything he had was tied up in the gyms and the dealership right now. He just didn't have the cash to rent somewhere else. And if he wanted the kids to stay longer than the odd weekend, he'd need at least three bedrooms. He couldn't be seen living in some skeevy place. He still had to lay low, and his business had taken a deep dip in sales. His wholesome family image had taken somewhat of a beating of late. Small towns were the worst. With the Internet, it was even tinier. People loved nothing better than seeing a successful man having his good name dragged through the damn mud. Cancel culture was expensive on the pocket when one was on the cull list.

Pulling up into his parking space at the dealership, he killed the engine and resisted the urge to call them again. They'd told him in no uncertain times to leave it, and he would know when the job was done.

The thing was, at this rate, he wouldn't have enough in his account to actually pay for what he'd ordered. Brittany was doing her best to drain his credit cards as it was, but he had to keep her sweet. What were those headshots again? Five hundred dollars? Then, there were the acting lessons, the lip fillers. His sweet little girlfriend was getting more expensive than the family he'd left her for.

Well, technically he had to leave, but that was just semantics. He was the man, and he needed to get back on top. The pressure was barreling down on him, and the letter from Bella's lawyer well and truly turned the screws. She was refusing to sell the house, citing that since she'd paid the deposit from the proceeds of her own place, and given that she was now paying the mortgage from her income, it was the family home and she would not entertain selling until their youngest was of college age. By which point, Gerald would be homeless, girlfriendless, and broke. She was so uppity, with her stupid romance books she called a career. Sure, they paid well, but he was the man. The winner of the bread. He was king, and he wanted to sell that castle so he could buy Brittany a new one. Having his kids with him would solve a lot of problems. No alimony for one. Not having to hear Brittany when she was on her broody rants. He already had enough kids, and if Brittany were to have them around full time, she'd soon stop talking about adding another baby to their load. He just needed to hold fast and make it happen.

A tap on his window jolted him. Brittany's smiling face filled the glass.

"Hey, baby, you coming in? The headshots arrived. They look amazing!"

Gerald suppressed the scream that threatened to engulf him, pushing it down into a low, rumbling sigh. Getting out of the car, he hugged her to him. "That's great, babe. Any appointments booked yet?"

She shrugged, obviously not caring. Even though it was her job to do the scheduling and monitor the appointments that his sales team made. She had never been that great at her job in the first place. Now that she was screwing the boss, her productivity had done nothing but diminish.

"No idea. Joe probably knows, you should ask him. I have that modelling agency appointment, remember?"

He looked at her blankly. "Is that today?"

She rolled her eyes, her thick lashes fanning wider. "Yes, babe, I told you. You got the registration fee, though, right?"

His chest clenched. There was that constricting pain again. He should get it looked at.

"How much was it again?" He pulled out his wallet, dismayed when he only saw a couple of fifties inside. "I might need to go to the bank."

She looked at the cash in his hand and shook her head. "It's, like, a thousand. I swear, Gerry baby, you don't listen!" She dropped a too quick kiss on his lips. "Never mind, I have the card. I'll just charge it."

Gerald smiled at her, but it felt more like a grimace. "Okay. I…er…better get to work."

The quicker this contract was fulfilled, the better. When Brittany had his kids to take care of and a house to clean, she'd have no time to spend all this money chasing dreams. His new life would be much more cost efficient.

CHAPTER
FIVE
BELLA

"Okay, well, two minutes okay? Then snuggle down. School tomorrow."

Bella padded down the stairs, purposefully walking past the shitshow of a kitchen in favor of the lounge. More specifically, the couch. Flouncing down on it, she flopped her head back on the overstuffed cushions, listening for the silence she longed for. She could hear her kids shuffling about upstairs, but the chaotic screeching and thumps were thankfully resigned to the past hour of hell. No wonder some parents called it the witching hour. Her kids were getting older, but it still took ages some afternoons to follow the bedroom routine they'd only had for, say, oh, all their lives.

The room she was in was only marginally better than the kitchen, she noted. There was an odd, dark brown stain on the couch cushion next to her that she prayed was Nutella from the toast her eldest had scoffed after declaring she was starving not half an hour after eating dinner. Crumbs littered the glass topped white wood coffee table she'd once thought was a must have for the room. In reality, the thing looked pretty, but she constantly banged her shins on it. It showed all the dirt and fingermarks, and she knew the crumbs currently strewn across its surface would be embedded in the cracks where the glass met the wood. A couple of times a month she had to get a hair pin and dig them out. Which was something else Gerald didn't appreciate.

Gerald *was* the damn coffee table, come to think of it. He'd looked pretty when they first met, with his perfect white teeth and the way his eyes drew her in. Now, she knew it was just because he had beady eyes that were just a little bit too close together. They *had* to draw you in, so you could even see him properly. She'd looked at him back then, just like she'd eyed the coffee table in the store. As a must have, something that would spark joy in her life. Well, that had backfired. Now, she was left to pick the crap out of the cracks, exhausted and fricking alone. Which was half the reason she'd agreed to date him in the first place all those years ago.

She'd been alone in her little apartment, trying to make it as a writer, tutoring to make rent, and utterly sick and jaded of the dating scene. Everyone had an agenda, it seemed–most of the men didn't want an ambitious, creative wife. They wanted someone who would dote on their every word, not someone who thought for themselves and wanted to share the chores equally. She was someone who talked to herself and had weekends where she declared she was going to take up a new hobby on a whim. Which she would then do, for hours on end. She still had those macrame plant potholders from the last obsession, hanging from hooks in the kitchen filled with trailing pathos. Gardening was another hobby she'd taken up, although that one was rather from necessity. Gerald wanted to pay a gardener an extortionate sum of money to mow the lawn and fill the beds with exotic plants. She'd put her foot down, telling him for a few hundred dollars she could do the garden, which she did. Lucky, really, since now she'd have to pay the gardener from the alimony he was constantly trying to wiggle out of paying. She wasn't even going after him for what she could, either, a fact that her lawyer kept reminding her when she had to speak to him. Her girlfriends said the same, but then they had the gardeners and the masseurs, the dog walkers and the therapists. She just didn't subscribe to that way of living. The once hard-up single gal in her just wouldn't allow it. Perhaps if she had, she wouldn't be the current laughing stock she was.

She sat there, contemplating her life until she heard nothing else from upstairs. They'd finally crashed out, and the night was hers. That thought depressed her more than thinking about her life. Gerald often worked late or sat in his office when he did come home, but she still knew he *was* coming home. Now, she wouldn't speak to another adult till the morning. No one to sit on the couch and watch TV with. No one to order take-out with or eat a late dinner. She could drink some wine, but she didn't want to get into that habit. She'd seen enough mothers on the PTA who seemed to talk about pinot just a little too affectionately. She couldn't afford a drinking habit right now. She could barely afford to keep the bills paid and still have something left till the next royalty check rolled in. Which was another source of depression.

Her agent was killer at her job, but lately she'd been piling on the pressure. The thing was, being in the public eye for the breakdown of her marriage and subsequent messy divorce wasn't the best advert for a bestselling romance writer. People always said writers needed to be tested through hardships, that trauma and misery made some of the best books, but all she could think was how futile it was to write about characters who took on the world and fell madly in love when she was stuck. Stuck in a life that was so different from the one she'd had. Looking back, she realized she wasn't even really happy with that life, but still. It would have been nice to have some choices in how things turned out.

Now, her agent wanted her to date again, and she wanted to buy sweatpants and start writing domestic noir thrillers instead. She'd even pitched an idea in that genre to her agent, but she'd just laughed and told her to take a night off and get out of the house. Which was all very well and good for her to say. She lived in the city where she could throw a stone and hit a book event to go to, or attend some art show with nibbles. Here in the suburbs, what was she going to do? Head to the local Arbee's and hang out there? Alone? Stick a pineapple upside down in her basket at the Piggly Wiggly? That seemed more of a Gerald thing to do. The man probably had a plethora of pineapples.

Suppressing a yawn, she pulled her phone out and fired up the dating app.

Constance had well and truly gone above and beyond her agent duties on this one. Sure, she'd been avoiding joining any of the apps, but signing up one's client? If they weren't such good friends, Bella would have deleted the data and fought her on it. But Constance had done a pretty good job. She made her sound almost dateable, which was more than Bella had come up with. And she'd only told her when there were messages there to be read. Which was a sound move, because if Constance had dropped the news on her with only an empty message inbox to show for her efforts, Bella might have thrown away all of her devices and joined a convent.

She brought up her inbox. She reread the message a man called John Smith had sent. Bit of a weird name, but then, she couldn't really talk. Her name was unusual enough to serve as a romance writer's pen name. So what if his name was a little nondescript? After Gerald Carmicheal, a calmer man might be just the ticket. She had to do something, if only to prove to Constance that all of this hassle regarding a new real life love interest wasn't going to pull her out of her writing slump.

The creative well, and her libido for that matter, were both dry. Dusty even. She had children to raise, the PTA to placate, pants to wash, and bills to pay. There were legal bills to pay, too, and if she lost that fight, she'd have to find a new home for her and her brood.

She hadn't had to resort to selling furniture yet, but she'd been eyeing up some of the designer bags Gerald had bought her over the years, wondering whether listing them online would benefit her any. Till the settlement and alimony was sorted, she didn't dare. She'd heard about other women who'd done such things to pay their bills and they'd been accused of disposing of assets, for selling things bought for them in the marriage. She wasn't even bothered about them, anyway. She'd never asked for designer gifts. Most of them she'd only used once for book events to keep up her secretive New Yorker persona, or to some work bash Gerald had brought her to. He always liked her to look the part, the woman dripping in wealth on his arm. A shiny little trophy, until he decided her gold surface was looking a little tarnished and decided to trade her in for a shinier new model.

"Well, here we go," she said aloud, clicking on John's profile. He was two years older than her. A consultant. His profile said Baltimore, which was promising. He'd listed his interests as travel, food, and reading. All big ticks, especially since most men on the app listed sports, beer, and the gym as their top three. At least they would have books in common.

His profile picture looked nice enough. From what she could see. The photo was taken from behind, so his facial features weren't visible. The slight side profile showed a strong jawline, his dark hair cut short and neat. He looked handsome, tanned, and tall. Well, he listed himself as over six feet. He could be a hobbit in real life, she supposed. Constance hadn't been completely honest on her profile, after all. If she had, it would have read more like a manic-depressive episode. *Stretchmarks, possible midlife crisis. Three spirited kids and an ex-husband hell bent on giving me gray hair and an early grave. My agent is making me do this to get my writing mojo back.*

No man was going to want that. She would swipe to swat away the male version of that, for sure. But Constance was right, she should at least try. She needed inspiration, something to take her out of her head a little. Besides, it was a message, not a marriage proposal.

Hey. Would love to chat with you.

For an opening message, it was pretty simple. A nice and easy introduction. She should reply. See what he was about. What else was she going to do with her evening, color coordinate her bookshelf? Spend another few hours rage cleaning with hard rock playing through her tear soaked headphones?

Eyeing the crumbs on the coffee table, she typed out, *Hi,* hitting send before she could second guess it.

Within seconds, she got one back.

Hi, how are you?

"Shit," Bella cursed. "How am I?" She tapped a finger on her lips, wondering how to make herself sound cool. Should she pretend to be out? At a wine bar maybe, or some gallery showing? On her profile, she was just listed as Bella. Perhaps, she didn't need to pretend to be the New York version of herself. Not here. Any suitor would figure it out, anyway, since Baltimore was listed as her location. Her profile pic was a candid shot, one Constance had taken after a long book tour day. She looked relaxed, hair down, laughing into the camera. It looked like the real her, so she decided that was what she was going to be. The real her, the one she still felt inside herself, hidden away.

Good, she typed instead. *What are you up to?*

The cursor kept moving, as if he was typing a long response. Then, it stopped. Started again. Was he deleting his answer?

I'd love to say I'm doing something exciting, but I landed a few hours ago so I'm just waiting for take-out before I fall asleep in front of the TV.

She chuckled at his answer. *Spend a lot of time travelling, do you, for work?*

Not for much longer, he wrote back. *Sort of working my notice at the minute.*

Interesting.

Consultant game not going well? She had no idea what a consultant was, to be fair. Whenever she heard the term, she thought of something generic. They seemed to have consultants in every field. Was he like George Clooney in that film, Up something? Flying in and closing down companies?

It's killer. Needed a change. What about you? Your profile never said what you did. I'm guessing you're an avid reader, though.

"Avid reader?" she muttered. "How would he know..." She looked back at her own profile, and with a groan, dialed her agent.

"Got some pages for me?"

"No. I'm working on it. That John Smith bio I screen-shotted to you. We've been messaging."

"Oh, nice!" Constance chipped in.

"Not nice. Weird. He thinks I'm a fan of, well, me."

"Come again?"

"The guy on this app you made me download. He thinks I'm a fan of Bella Carmichael. Why did you say in the bio I read books like Bella Carmichael?"

"Well, I wanted to talk you up! Some guys don't like women reading those upbeat feminine reads, you know? Thought it might weed them out."

"It makes me look like a narcissist, Con!"

"Nooo!" She chuckled, and Bella could hear her heels walking on the sidewalk. The woman was always hustling, always at some New York event or another. "If they meet you, it will be funny! And I told you to let me put a better picture on. You look totally different to your author photos, so the average Joe is hardly likely to realize it's you, are they? If it bothers you, show them one of your book jacket photos."

"Oh yeah, like I'm going to now! What if he's a nutball?"

"What if he is? That's why you follow the dating rules. Meet him in public, tell people where you are, have your location on your phone for friends. I have the log-ins for the app. I can check them out if you're worried."

"That won't help if he knows who I am, though!"

"Girl, you're overthinking this. The world thought you lived in New York, before the…" She trailed off, and Bella knew she was referring to the very public affair and divorce scandal. And the fact that her daughter had outed her own father online to the world as a cheating hog. "The point is, your bio says you live in Baltimore, and it doesn't sound like you. You want the guy to like your books, right? It's a big part of you! It's a conversation, that's all. He's going to know who you are eventually! No one dates these days without googling first. It's why I kept your surname off there. Besides, he's called John Smith. He's probably a right bore. Just think of him as a test run."

Bella thought back to his profile picture. "He doesn't look

like a bore. One of the photos he posted was on a mountain top."

"Photoshop. He probably did it at the library." A cackle came down the line. "Or in his mother's basement. But people do this every day, online dating is the way forward now. Social media is it. Just pick a guy, and stay safe. Go on a date already, and then send me the deets."

"Fine," Bella pouted. "If I end up dismembered or kidnapped, I will blame you."

"Fine, I'll console myself with the book sales it will generate. Night."

"Night," Bella laughed, returning to the message. Should she just fess up straightaway? She armed herself with a glass of cold white wine before replying.

I am as it goes. You've read Bella Carmichael?

Oh yeah, he typed back. *Everyone loves a good romance, right? She's a master of her craft.*

Wow. If only he knew. The three dots danced across the screen again.

Speaking of romance, I would like to meet you.

"Wow, straight in." She took a steadying sip of wine, typing back before she could stop herself. Something about this guy made her feel comfortable. Intrigued. She wanted to know more. *Maybe I should google him.* That was what people did, right? Except his name was John Smith, which was not exactly easy to narrow down. *He might google me when he knows who I am.* Shit. Googling her was *very* easy to narrow down. She was out there, for her books, and she knew that somewhere on the Internet would be the story of her divorce, and her kids. He needed to know what he was getting into. Not the full story, but the main part. The important stuff.

Sounds good, although I will warn you. I do have chil-

dren. I am separated, and have been single for a little while now.

She drank more wine, waiting for the inevitable blocking, when his message pinged back.

Going through a divorce, huh? You okay?

She had no hesitation on that one.

Yep. Glad it happened. Just me and the kids now. She took another slurp, feeling the wine warm her. Liquid courage. *I have three.*

Three? Nice. Boys, girls?

Eldest is a boy, and two girls. You can block me now. No hard feelings.

No blocking, he typed back. *I like kids. At our age, everyone has something in their lives. Thanks for telling me. I'd love to hear more about them when you are ready. I would still like to take you out.*

Bella blushed into her glass. His reply made her smile. He was either full of shit, or incredibly sincere. Constance's words were still in the back of her mind. She needed this. It was a step forward. A new experience to write about, if nothing else. The kids would be gone before she could blink, and then what? She needed to try to move on. If only to get her out of her sweat pant streak. Constance was pushy, but she was also right. Gerald had moved on before their marriage had ended. She deserved to see what was out there, and what life post the cheating jerk might look like.

I'd like that, too, She typed back with vino fueled fingers. *This might be my first date in over a decade, so bear with me.*

Snap. Travelling around the world for work is all well and good, but it makes you wary of people. No expectations. Just drinks if you like, or a meal if you feel daring. I'm in Baltimore for a while. No travels planned any time soon. I would like to get to know you. No pressure, of course. Just two people meeting up.

A meal sounded nice. Gerald usually just took her out to networking events, and they had a standing table at the local Italian restaurant for their anniversary. This would be something else new. An actual event with food that didn't come in dinosaur shapes or with a free toy, in a nice setting with other grown-ups.

Sure, we could do that, she wrote. *When?*

———

John's lip curled up at her reply. She'd agreed to meet. Bella Carmichael, the woman whose books had kept him company on some dark, cold nights, was going out with him. He'd decided the second he'd seen her profile that it was important. Serendipity, somehow. Even before the job, he'd been invested in the woman. The only reason he hadn't done a deep dive on her before was that he didn't want to find out she was some horrible person deep down, or happily settled down. *Never meet your heroes, right?* The not knowing of personal things about her made her all the more mysterious.

When the scandal about her husband broke, he'd felt so mad on her behalf, but it still wasn't his business. Bella lived in a very different world to him. The real world. Marriage, mortgages, families, and BBQs in the backyard. All things he had never had, but now found himself craving. Bella and he were never going to meet, their paths were too far away to ever cross.

Until Gerald's contract brought her screaming into his world, unbeknown to her.

Finding out that her agent had set up a dating profile at

the same time? It was perfect. Meant to be, in a twisted kind of way. His way in, to hopefully get close and keep her safe.

He wouldn't have taken the job at all if it hadn't been her. Not only did she not fit his work criteria, but her ex-husband was also a piece of work. He'd known it the second he'd heard about him. He was a selfish coward, and the polar opposite to everything John stood for. So, he'd taken the job. For her. What else was he going to do, but see this thing through?

I am pretty flexible with work. You pick the place and time, and I'll be there. Looking forward to meeting you, Bella.

When she sent him a pin with the location, he grinned. He knew just where the place was. She was letting him in, he realized. He was about to enter Bella's life properly. Now, he just hoped he could pull this off. Getting Bella to like him enough to keep him around would make keeping her alive that much easier.

If he could keep his damn heart in check. Messaging her, seeing her vulnerability through her messages–it was endearing. He wanted to dive deep into her head and know everything there was to know about her.

Being part of her world, and preserving it, would be worth the deception. It would balance his books. End his career on the best high. The world needed Bella Carmicheal in it. He needed Bella in the world. Then, he could retire in peace, knowing he'd keep his mark alive. How it should be. The easiest job in the world. He never lost sleep over a job, but failing to keep Bella alive would haunt his damn dreams.

He typed back a reply, wishing he could see her face when she saw it. *Perfect. See you soon Bella. Looking forward to it. Sweet dreams.*

Me too, she typed back. *Have a good night.*

When his room service arrived, he thanked the bell boy and returned with it to his desk.

Contact made, he messaged to Hannah. *Any contact from the client, let me know.*

Affirmative, Hannah typed back. *Radio silence till I hear from you. Good luck, Mr. Black.*

Turning back to Bella's profile, he scrutinized the photo again. It didn't look like her book jacket photographs, but it was definitely her. She looked lighter on the profile picture, more comfortable in her own skin. Her face was glowing, her expression captured mid laugh. She was beautiful. The more he saw of her, the more intrigued he became. The public persona was so far removed from the woman in this photo, and the woman he'd seen at the gas station. Three different women.

It made him wonder who the real Bella Carmichael was. He felt like he knew her from reading her books. The beautiful prose, the way she crafted her characters.

When the scandal broke, it was her husband the news focused on. His wealth, the Baltimore empire he had built. The pretty girlfriend he had been seeing behind her back. She'd had some two-bit role as a cadaver in a crime show the year before, and she was often on social media making videos about make-up and wanting to be a big star. Little was mentioned about Bella herself, or her children. When he'd investigated, he'd found that a lot of it had been scrubbed from the internet, so her agent must have been earning her commission. He'd had to hack the dark web to find the information, and even some of that was missing. Bella had stayed silent on the subject in the press, and eventually the gossip mill had died down. Although, being in Andersen Falls, he knew the people around here would have long memories. He'd never spent much time in small, close-knit places like these, but his online diving had shown that people were not above gossiping about their neighbors.

The haunted look on Bella's face at the gas station made sense to him. Like a startled goldfish in a tapped bowl, she was spooked. The worst part, he was sure, would have been how the whole thing came out. It made him admire the woman even more. Her taking a step into the dating pool? It had to have taken a lot, even if, through his hacking of her emails, he knew her agent was the impetus behind it. The fact that she was stuck in her life, her career, whilst not even knowing someone was trying to end it? It made his blood boil. Which led him back to the problem. Gerald Carmichael. He turned to his laptop screen, reading through the latest accounts of the Carmicheal businesses.

"Hmm." He took a bite of the burger he'd ordered. "Looks like the people of Baltimore are not keen on cheaters. Go figure." Since the date of the scandal hitting online, his businesses had been on a downturn. Gym memberships were down across all three of his gyms, and the dealership was close to the red. "No wonder you need to trim the fat, buddy boy."

Over-extended was not the word. Other than the house, which had ten years left on the mortgage, everything was levied. Remortgaged. The gyms in Chesapeake and Washington were losing money, and the payments and wages were just about being met. The car dealership was smoke and mirrors. Some of the cars on his lot were total ringers, the sticker prices being well over market value. He was paying his half of the mortgage, but taking it straight out of the business accounts rather than his personal account. The guy was mooching off his mother by living in her house with his girlfriend, and the spending on his credit cards read like he was Rockefeller. High-end boutiques, nice meals out–half of which were put through as business expenses. He was shorting his way through the money, and with Bella still being married to him on paper, the house was in jeopardy. Which was precisely why he was pushing her for less alimony payments and the sale of the house. He had fifty thousand dollars in an obscure account that was hidden in some tax shelter, but it wouldn't last. In six months' time, he would be out of money and the wolves at the door were already peeing on the wood to mark their territory. None of which Bella knew, because the schmuck was giving the lawyers the bare minimum in paperwork and what he was sending to them was so fabricated it made Harry Potter sound like a documentary on the school system.

The fact was, he couldn't even afford to pay the hitman fees once Bella was dead. Which would ordinarily be a problem if he had any intention of killing her. The twenty thousand dollar deposit for his services had cleared, but the secret account worried him. If he didn't get results soon, he'd have more money to play with to get the job down. Desperate times called for desperate measures with people like him, and greed and control went hand in hand.

"Geez," he huffed, chomping a now lukewarm fry. "It's easier to take people out than it is to keep them alive. I have a new respect for Costner. No wonder he was so grumpy with Whitney in that movie."

Bella's accounts were much cleaner. She now had her royalties put into her own account, instead of the joint one, but a lot of it had gone into the business, too, over the years. The fact was, Bella was doing well, but she would have been doing a hell of a lot better if Gerald hadn't been in charge of the finances. Now, with the meager payments she was getting from him and no other income but her own, things were going to be tight. She needed the next book to do well, because relying on Gerald to settle things was never going to happen.

"Fucker," John spat, pushing his food aside. He dialed Hannah.

"Mr. Black?"

"Hey. I need you to go book shopping. Make the sales look legit."

The line was quiet for half a second. "What did your last personal shopper die of?"

"I killed them for being sarcastic," he quipped back. "Use my accounts, but funnel it through legit channels. I need it to equal twenty thousand dollars in royalties."

"Twenty thousand, huh? Same as the deposit Mr. Carmichael paid. Interesting. I take it he fudged the accounts?"

"You take it right. So, can you do it?"

"I don't know, but I'll figure it out."

"Buy a damn bookstore if you have to, just make sure the sales go through rapidly. I don't need to know the costs, but I need the payment to filter through her agent quickly and not raise her suspicions. The two of them are pretty close, and I don't want to raise any flags."

"Money situation is that bad, huh? I knew he was a slimy git. Any particular book? War and Peace, perhaps?"

"Cute. You know which ones." He tapped a couple of keys, scrolling down to find what he was looking for. "Also, I'll be giving the dummy number to a letting agent. They'll need the usual references, through the consulting company cover."

"Done. Can I ask why you're giving your deposit to the mark?"

"You can," he smiled, "but if I tell you…"

"You'll have to kill me." He could hear her amused smirk through the phone. "Roger that. Over and out, Black."

"Thanks, Hannah." Scrolling through the options Andersen Falls had to offer, he stopped at a listing that was close to Bella's house and sent an email to the agent. If he was going to be sticking around and taking Bella out on dates, he needed to stop living out of a suitcase. He didn't know which one he was happier about, but he slept like a log the second his head hit the pillow.

CHAPTER
SIX
BELLA

Book idea: Suburban man goes full-on Carrie at the PTA bake sale.
Buy pantyhose.
Burn sweatpants?

The school moms were at the gate, looking like an American Spice Girls tribute band. The leader of them all, 'Posh Spice' Chrissie, clocked Bella's approach with the kids and nudged the others.

God, they are like vultures circling. Vultures mixed with hyenas, all cackles and picking meat from the bones of all around them.

"Hi, Bella!" She grinned like a Stepford wife. The other witches in the coven all turned to watch her approach.

Bella was juggling book bags and lunchboxes. Evan was moaning at the side of her about being late for registration, and she shushed him desperately. She knew she should have used the carpool lane, but Poppy had nagged about being tardy, and the line was always long close to bell time.

Since the whole online scandal, Poppy had been a little

clingier than usual. Bella missed the bright, bubbly kid who ran out of the car the second she'd parked, dashing off to meet her friends. This generation had it much harder with the Internet knowing every little thing. In her day, they still did plenty of dumb shit, and their parents still had affairs, pill addictions, and gambling habits. The difference was, no one had anywhere to post about it, and every person didn't have a camera phone in their pocket ready to capture the humiliation in high definition.

"Mom," Evan moaned. "If I'm late for registration, my tutor will tell the coach. You're buying me extra laps here!"

"Evan, give me a minute. Please." She turned to the coven and flashed what she hoped looked like a relaxed smile. "Hello, ladies." Before she took another step, she felt a hand on her arm.

"How are you doing? We haven't seen much of you around town."

Yeah, Bella thought with a huff. *Because I've been avoiding gossiping shit mongers like you.* She was still smarting from the supermarket encounter.

"No, well, you know how it is." She waved her arm, trying to be breezy. The book bag missed Chrissie's nose by a whisker. "Busy, busy! Kids and deadlines."

"Oh," Prunella simpered. "You're really writing a new book?"

Bella frowned. "Er, yeah, it's kind of my job. You know us working moms, always on the go!"

Prunella's lips pursed. Damn it, she'd awoken the dragon. Prunella didn't work. Hadn't since the week after her honeymoon with Bill, when she'd come home and handed in her notice to 'concentrate on other things'. Those other things seemingly consisted of judging people, having children every three years, and ruling the PTA with an iron fist that scared most of the school, including Principal Danvers. It wasn't the fact she chose not to work that was the problem. Bella just hated the way she used it in a way to make the other mothers feel inadequate for not making individually themed cupcakes for every bake sale, or for not being able to be at every celebration and assembly. Fathers didn't do this to each other, did they?

Maybe her next book should be about motherhood, she mused as Prunella's lips kept flapping.

"Bella, you in there? Yoo hoo!"

Her kids, sensing the situation, had grabbed the contents of her arms and headed off through the gates.

Great, the first time the kids hadn't moaned about going to school, and now I can't get away.

"Sorry," she started to say, before realizing she didn't actually need to apologize. "Busy day," she said through her gritted teeth smile. "See you later."

"Oh, before you go," Chrissie cut in. "I just wondered, you've not signed up for anything yet on the events calendar? You missed the meeting, so I emailed you the details."

Bella wracked her brain and her email recollection. She remembered seeing something, but she got so many school-related emails she'd just brushed it to one side. "Er, no. Been busy, you know."

Prunella's nostrils flared, just for a second. Perfectly in sync with the eye twitch Chrissie tried and failed to stop. If she'd blinked she would have missed it, but Bella clocked their irritation and stored the information away for a future date. Maybe these twitches were like Pokémon cards. She wondered what her reward would be if she scored the full set. Angela and Meredith, standing on the fringes of the pride of lionesses, were openly staring. She kept her eyes firmly on the ugly inside sisters.

"Well, you really do need to sign up for something!" The quartet all nodded in unison. The visual was downright eerie, even in couture.

"Why?" She blurted it out before she could stop herself. "Why do I need to sign up for things?"

Angela made a funny squeaking sound, and Chrissie looked like the vein in her forehead was about to pop. "What do you mean, why? Because, uh, the PTA!"

"It's for the children," Prunella chipped in. "Don't you want to help your children?"

Her phone pinged in her hand, and she saw John's name pop up. *Hope your day is going well, Bella. Looking forward to our date. Kick some ass.*

Kick some ass. He had no idea how much she wanted to hear that right now. It was exactly what she wanted to tick off her list today. She popped her hip, then showed them some teeth.

"I do help my children, Pru. I take them to school, I cook, and I clean. I work my tush off to provide for them, and I take them to all their activities and extracurriculars. I pay my bills, and on a daily basis I refrain from screaming into a pillow when they drive me nuts. And since when does a mom need to join the PTA, anyway? Where are the dads in all this? Do they sit and make banners for school dances, or stay up till 2am baking bespoke cupcakes, Angela? I have been part of this school for a while now, and when Evan first joined, I did all of that. I even sewed sequins on costumes for the winter play. My fingers were so sore by the end of that weekend, I couldn't type. I've done my bit, and I don't see every mom in the school helping out."

Chrissie's face had steadily turned red, shade by shade. "That's hardly the point. Not every mom cares enough to put the time in."

"Yeah?" She laughed, feeling so free she wanted to do a high kick. "Well, why don't you go ahead and add me to that list. Have a good day, ladies."

She turned on her heel, managing to make it two steps before Chrissie spoke. "Well, I would have thought that fostering friendships would be important, given everything your family is going through. I mean, Gerald is cavorting all over town with his pretty new girlfriend, and the way Daisy is going with her computer skills, she is bound to be on the Pentagon watch list by the time she graduates. And poor little Poppy, she doesn't even know what gender to be!"

Bella snapped back around so fast she almost lost her footing. "Chrissie, why don't you just–"

She raised a manicured finger, waggling it in Bella's face. "Now, now. We just worry about you, that's all! You have to admit, Poppy's choice of clothing–"

"The boy jeans, and the T-shirts," Meredith added, looking gleeful at throwing a barb into the mix.

"Oh I know, and the sneakers? My Austin has the same pair," Angela smirked, the other women all agreeing.

"We worry she's confused, you know. There's a lot of influences on children nowadays, and without a father at home…"

Bella unclenched her teeth before the enamel cracked. "Poppy knows who she is, ladies. My children are fine, and if they weren't, you would be the last people I would come to for advice." She stomped off, before changing her mind and storming back. The ladies stepped backward, eyes wide. "And take me off the email list, too. You have too much time on your hands, and it's clogging up my inbox."

"We're just trying to help!" Angela, the meeker of the group, called after her.

"Help this." Without a backward glance, she flipped them

the finger over her shoulder and got the hell out of there. "Have a fantastic day, ladies!"

As she strode away, she saw Daisy's friend's mom standing nearby, open mouthed. Putting her head down, she focused on getting to the car park without crying.

"About time someone did that," Trudie called out. "Good for you, Bella."

Good for me, she agreed. It was about time she started to kick some ass. That comment, and the text from John, held off the tears until she put the key in her front door. *Baby steps,* she told herself. *One enemy at a time.*

CHAPTER
SEVEN
JOHN

John slid silently into the passenger seat. The man behind the steering wheel jumped, and it gave John the tiniest thrill to see it. He'd been scoping out the parking lot for the last two hours, checking every angle, and monitoring the traffic. When Jasper had asked for the meeting, he knew it was because of the job. The last job he ever planned to take. He'd been expecting it. Jasper was a control freak, and the closest thing he had ever had to a father. And like all good fathers, he wanted the best for his son. Unfortunately, in this case, the best was for him to stay on the payroll, and Daddy Dearest wasn't used to not getting his way. John didn't want to sour their relationship, but he needed to make him understand it was a done deal. He needed things to go by the book. Get his shot at living a normal life, out of the shadows. He didn't want to have any loose ends.

Clean and clear. No casualties.

"Losing your touch, Jasper. I could have popped you off three or four different ways."

"But you won't," Jasper's gravelly voice rumbled back. John could barely make out his side profile in the dark. He was wearing his usual brimmed hat, collar turned high on his coat. Someone you wouldn't pick out of a line-up. That was the point. "You need me for your exit plan."

John's jaw clenched. "I've earned my retirement."

"Early retirement," Jasper countered. "Which we both know doesn't happen in our line of work. What makes you different? What makes you think you won't get bored in a year and beg me to come back?"

"Nothing makes me different. I'm just done. That's the point. It's been done before. You did it. You can do it for me."

"And lose my best agent in the field?"

"Flattery, Jasper?" He turned to look at his handler. "What's next, a pay raise? Employee of the month? Ooh, do I get a certificate, a plaque on the wall?"

A car drove past, high beams lighting up the windshield. Both men followed its movement.

"Jackass," they said in unison.

The car grew silent once more.

"I want this, Jasper. I'm tired of the life. I won't want to come back. It doesn't mean I'm not grateful for what you did for me."

"You did the work. All I did was take you off the street and show you a different way to get your life back." He sighed, as if the news was just settling in for him. "If this is what you want, I can make it happen, but there will be rules."

"I know."

"Secrets must be kept. No freelancing. Retirement, early or otherwise, is not usually our company policy."

"Yeah," John muttered. "Because the employees don't even get there most of the time. The pension pot at the agency is hardly in threat of going dry. I know the rules, you wrote them. I want out. All the way out. The only thing I want to keep from my illustrious career is my name."

"Bit of a dull name to keep," Jasper countered, his voice cool and steely. "Has this got something to do with the last job you took? I see it's still in the in-tray."

"It doesn't fit the criteria."

"Exactly. The money is not what you usually command, either." Jasper turned to look at him for the first time. "Which was why I was surprised you even took it on. You know what you're doing there?"

John grinned, his teeth flashing white in the dark of the night. "For the first time in my life, no clue. It feels pretty good, this retirement lark."

Jasper said nothing, but John was pretty sure he saw a little smirk. "We'll see. I thought the same when I quit the killing game. Yet, here I am. Still doing it. We're the same, you and I. I knew it the minute I met you. Back when you were that angry kid on the street. Mundanity will kill you faster than any bullet ever could."

"Yeah? Well, I've been shot, and it's a hell of a lot more painful than a Sunday reading the papers. I want this, Jasp. I'm not changing my mind. When the job's over, I'm done. Out."

He watched his mentor slowly nod his head, wondering when all those lines appeared on his face. Had so much time really passed since that day on the street? It felt like a lifetime, and the map of their escapades was visible in the crags on his skin.

"We'll talk again. When this Carmichael business has been…resolved. I do hope you know what you're doing on that one. It's messy. And I don't like being messy."

John pulled open the car door. "Yeah, well, I'll do the exit interview, but this is not messy. It's different, this one. I don't need the money, and you're hardly hurting for an influx of cash."

"I know who she is, John. The mark."

John felt the cold steel under his clenching fist as he looked back into the car. "She's not a mark. Call her that again and we'll have a problem."

Jasper raised a brow. "I thought so. Business and pleasure don't mix. You really going to do this because you like reading her stupid books? Maybe I need to get Jennings on this, or outsource."

"I'm warning you, Jasper. I know where the bodies are buried, remember?"

"Yeah, you do. You put half of them in the ground yourself."

"Yeah, well, a couple more won't matter, then. It's not about the books, and you know it. This is the last time I'll warn you to stay out of my business."

"John–"

"No. Mentor or not, I will fuck you up if you go anywhere near Bella. Understood?"

The glare he got back confirmed he'd made his point. "Fine. Keep your phone on. I might have other jobs come up. You're still in until this is over."

"I'm not doing any more hits."

"Yeah." Jasper's smile was feral. "Well, once your job ends, so does your employment contract. Up to you when that is, isn't it? Pop, pop, and done. You'd be free and clear."

John shook his head, his jaw clenching so tight he felt like his face might crack in two. "Bye, Jasper."

"Call me," his sarcastic voice called back, just as John slammed the door in his face.

CHAPTER
EIGHT
BELLA

With everything she had going on with the kids, and the back and forth with Gerald's solicitors, Bella had been busy. Not busy writing, but still.

Tonight might just remedy that.

She'd finally agreed to go out with John, after cancelling on him twice. Constance was screaming for pages, but the screen on her computer was still blank. The white glare taunted her every time she looked at it, and the days on the calendar were falling away far faster than she would have liked. Her email inbox was a little lighter since the PTA had backed off, but she knew it wasn't over. The looks she got when she saw them around town gave her an uneasy feeling. Which she felt in the pit of her stomach right now, just for a very different reason.

"Are you sure you're going to be okay? I can cancel. I'd still pay you, of course."

Erin, her longstanding babysitter and a college freshman, was having none of it. She had one hand on Bella's back and one on the kitchen door.

"Yes, for the tenth time, I'm sure," she said with a pointed shove. "Come on, you deserve a night out, and we'll be fine! The kids are comfy in front of the TV. We have a Disney marathon planned for later. Daisy coded a new game she wants to show me, and Evan and Poppy are watching the rest of the game." She gently pushed her again, but Bella dug her heels in. "Mrs. Carmichael."

"Yeah?" Bella was well aware that her whole body was rigid, but she was in full-on panic mode. Every time she tried to get her feet to work, her knees knocked together. Of all the questionable life choices she'd made over the years, she decided that this had to be top ten at least.

"Do you not want to go on this date?"

"Of course I do!" she squeaked back, looking her fresh-faced teenage babysitter in the face for the first time since she'd arrived an hour earlier. "Why do you think I don't?"

Erin deadpanned back, "The fact you're clinging to the dishwasher for dear life?"

Bella's fingers unlocked the second she was called out. "Touche." Popping her head out the door, she could see the children in the other room. They were all watching the TV, wide-eyed and occasionally moving to shove popcorn into their half open mouths. Just seeing them all sitting together helped slow her racing heartbeat. Heading back into the kitchen, she headed straight for the fridge and pulled out the corked bottle of white wine from the other night. Erin reached into the clean dishwasher and passed her a glass.

"Thanks," she smiled. "Sorry I lost my mind there."

"I understand." Erin took a seat on one of the breakfast bar stools. "When my mom got divorced, she was the same. Worse, actually. She spent a whole week in her dressing gown and then flashed the gardener."

Bella didn't know what to think of that, given Erin had been her neighbor for the past fifteen years. Erin's mom was the type of woman who always trimmed up her house better than anyone else on the street and made homemade gifts for the mail carrier. Poor Derek, too. She knew the gardener in question, and he was a mild mannered Texan in his sixties. *I wonder if the cowboy hat he always wore had fallen off at the sight of his client showing him her lady parts.*

"Sorry, I didn't know. Sounds rough, and I get it." *Another reason to be glad I do my own gardening.*

"Yeah," Erin shrugged it off, but Bella could see the pain behind it. "It was pretty awkward. She gave him a big tip that month. She still blushes when they cross paths."

"I bet it was hard for you, too, seeing your mom go through that. I wish I'd known."

"I didn't like to talk about it. It was bad enough at school. You know how people talk."

"Yeah, I do." Understatement of the year.

Erin's face fell. "Oh God, I didn't mean–"

"I know you didn't," Bella soothed her with a warm smile. "I'm glad I found out. I just kind of wish it hadn't been quite so public. I felt like Sandra Bullock at the beginning of that film, the one where she moves back home after being jilted and falls in love with a Southern crooning cowboy." Erin's face was blank. "Your mother will know it. Anyway, it happened. Daisy was protecting me. The important thing is that the kids are okay." She bit at her lip before realizing it was slicked in lipstick. "Shit." She reached for her bag to check her reflection in her compact mirror. A pale face with lipstick smeared teeth stared back. "Great. I look like a toddler playing dress-up."

Erin laughed, coming over. "I'll fix it. Paper towels?"

Bella pointed to the dispenser on the counter. "Thanks. I can't remember the last time I went on a date. I–"

The doorbell rang. Both women squeaked.

"He's here." Bella's voice came out high enough for only dogs to hear. When Erin had fixed her make-up, she took a deep breath. "Thanks. Listen, anything happens with the kids, a power cut, anything…"

"We'll be fine. Unless lightning strikes the house, you have no reason to come home. My mom's next door, anyway." Bella didn't move. The doorbell rang again. "Er." Erin looked toward the hallway. "You have to actually answer the door for the date to start."

"This is a bad idea," Bella protested, her heeled feet locked to the floor. "It's too soon."

"It's dinner." Erin gave her a gentle push. "Not a marriage proposal. Worst case scenario, you send me an SOS text. I'll call you with a fake explosive diarrhea issue, and you come home."

"Explosive diarrhea?"

"Yeah." She winked. "No man would ask questions about that one. You come home, and call my mom. She can come over and bring wine." Her face lit up with a smirk. "She got dad's wine collection in the settlement, so I'm sure she would love to use some of it to cheer up a fellow divorcee."

Bella felt her nerves subside a little. "You're too smart for your age, you know that?"

Erin laughed, giving her another, stronger shove toward the front door. "I know. I get it from my mom. Now, go. You look great, and you deserve this. Don't worry about a thing here. We're good."

Bella nodded dumbly. It wasn't her kids she was worried about. She was going to fire Constance first thing in the morning.

———

John watched the shadow get bigger against the lights in the hallway. A second later, the door opened, and there she was. Her photographs had *not* done her justice. Being a former sniper, he'd always prided himself on being able to slow his breathing, maintain his oxygen levels. That all went out the window the instant they locked eyes. He had to urge his lungs to inflate and order his heart to beat again.

"Hi," she said shyly, offering him a little smile he wanted to put in his pocket to stay with him forever.

"Hello, Bella," he managed to get his vocal cords to croak out. "You ready?"

He wanted to tell her she looked beautiful, but he forced himself to wait. She could still change her mind and shut the door in his face. Judging from the panicked emails she'd been sending Constance, it was a miracle she hadn't cancelled again. Luckily, he was a patient man when it came to getting his way, but the startled deer look on her pretty face had his nerves jangling. There was still time for her to pull out of this. He needed her to leave the house. More than he needed to breathe at this point, it seemed.

"Sure." She eyed the flowers in his hands, reminding him he was holding the blooms.

"These are for you. Flowers." *Nice one. She can see that, dufus.*

"Yes, they are," she giggled. Her fingers went to her lips, silencing it before she reached for the cellophane clad bouquet. "Thank you." A young girl appeared over her shoulder. The neighbor's kid and babysitter, Erin. He'd already checked out her neighbors and the people in her life. It was standard for any job he undertook. Aside from smoking a little weed with her friends on the weekend, Erin was clean. Her mother had a predilection for uniform porn on the net, but otherwise the household of Bella Carmichael was in pretty safe hands for the night.

Bella herself was now in his hands. No threats would come near her while he drew breath.

He couldn't help but pick up on her shaking hands as she moved, and he wanted to grasp them. To still her quaking. Maybe even replace it with a tremble of his own making.

"Are you all right?" he asked before he could stop himself. He wanted to know every facet of her.

Man, I am a goner. Focus, Mr. Black.

Right now, he felt more vulnerable than he ever had before. He hadn't felt like this since he was that discarded kid, living rough and reading her books for something to comfort him. She'd written about a character just like him, but in that story he'd met a girl who took him in. Changed his destiny. Loved him back to life. It had kept him warmer than any blanket, and the slight obsession for her words had never quite left his heart.

"You seem a little stressed." He didn't offer her an out. In case she took it.

"Yeah." She clenched her fingers tight, and he clocked the ringless left hand. "Yes, I'm good." The air she puffed out from her cheeks made her hair flutter around her face. Lit up from the hallway lights, it was a pretty sexy move. Vulnerable. Cute. *I might be in trouble here,* he mused before shifting his focus back to laser. "Sorry. First date since…" She bit down on her bottom lip. *Well, she would have to stop that right now.* "It's been a while." Her eyes bulged at her unintentional double entendre. "At dating!" The teen snickered from down the hall, and Bella's eyes closed as her cheeks filled with blood. All this cute lip biting nervousness was filling a part of him with the red stuff, too. "At dating, I meant. Not that I haven't…or have! Oh God. Erin!" She practically squeaked the babysitter's name whilst grasping for the door handle. "I won't be late!"

"Okay!" Erin called back before the door closed, leaving the two of them alone on the porch. "Shall we go?" Eying the camera on her doorbell, he nodded, holding out his arm for her to take.

"Let's do it."

Tonight was a first for him, too. Probably in a few more ways than Bella. Definitely in more ways than she could know about. The research alone was work. He had to know who was in their immediate world. Who and what might see him. The suburbs were a breeding ground for dash cams, door cameras, and security. His recon had been thorough. He could hack his image away by the time it took to make a cup of coffee. What he hadn't banked on was how real it would feel when he got here. How much this non-date idea of protection would feel like a date. His palms were sweaty, for fuck's sake. Holding a sniper rifle had never generated anything like the damp fever his hands felt. Being in her presence again made it all the harder to pretend this was fake for him at all. It was a…complication.

Pulling his head out of his thoughts, he saw she was still standing there, hand still glued to her front door.

"Ready?" he checked.

"I'm still deciding," she said back, as if the words had slipped from her mouth unbidden.

He cocked his head to one side, nodding at the handle she was white knuckling. "Honest," he stated. "I like it. It might be easier to move if you let go of the handle, though."

She was gnawing at that lip again. He wanted to step forward and free it from the enamel prison she was keeping it trapped in. But then he'd want to do other things, so he waited. Luckily for him, patience was one of his stronger virtues and he had nowhere else to be. Nowhere else he wanted to be.

A movement on the street caught his peripheral. He didn't move an inch. They weren't alone. They needed to move, one way or the other.

"Maybe we should do this another time." She'd go back inside, and he'd deal with any threats. He went to leave, and her hand let go of the handle. A second later, he felt her fingers slip into the crook of his tense forearm.

"I'm ready," she said with more conviction in her voice than he'd heard before. "Wow, you feel as coiled up as I feel."

"I guess we're both on edge." Hand placed over hers, he led her to his waiting vehicle.

He clocked the car across the street and logged the plates in his memory. Hmm. It seemed the ex was a voyeur as well as an asshole. Had he heard about their date? Other than Constance, Bella kept her world small. That left the hit. He was waiting for it and wanted a front row seat. John tamped down his anger, loosening his taut body so his companion wouldn't pick up on the tension.

"Where are we going?"

"Oh, you'll like it," he confirmed. "It's a nice place."

As he saw her to the passenger seat, he turned purposefully and shot a long look at the windscreen of the peeper before leaning into the car.

"Here," he breathed, his voice thick with the suppressed rage pounding through him. "Let me." He reached for her belt, his stubble brushing against her cheek as he gently pulled it across her body. He heard the click as it slid home, and the hitch in her breath at his proximity. "Safe and secure," he muttered before pulling back and eyeing the car with a raised brow. Pulling out his phone, he snapped a quick pic just as the car's lights lit up. Putting the handset to his ear as he walked around the back of the car, he eyed the vehicle the whole way. Once it hit the stop sign at the end of the street and turned left, he opened the driver's side door and pretended he was on a call.

"That's fine, Wendy. Thanks. I won't be taking any calls for the rest of the evening." He paused. "Great, thanks. See you tomorrow."

"Everything okay?"

"Not a worry in the world," he smiled. "Just work. We won't be disturbed again." As he drove away, watching her hands relax a little in her lap, it broadened. "Let's go get a drink. I want to hear all about my date."

CHAPTER
NINE
BELLA

John took her to the café she'd mentioned for their first date. He didn't even baulk when they pulled up, even though he looked like the type of man who frequented five-star restaurants that didn't do anything crass like putting the prices on the menu. He'd led her to a booth without a glimmer of unease, and they'd ordered grilled cheese sandwiches and fries, washed down with one of Café Eleven's signature thick shakes. It had been easy, and the pressure she'd felt seeing him at the door had fallen away pretty quickly. He'd asked about her kids. She'd told him the sorry story of how Daisy's Internet skills had discovered her father's affair. How she'd hacked his Facebook page and outed him and Brittany. How the local and national news had picked up on the story. How she'd found out the morning after, waking up to a million notifications and a panicking, sniveling Gerald. Daisy had thought she was doing the right thing. A woman scorned was a lesson she'd learned early.

He'd listened to everything without cutting her off or commenting. For the first time in a long time, she'd felt listened to.

"Wow. You really weren't kidding about just moving in."

His brow lifted as he closed his front door behind them. She'd barely stepped past the entrance, and as his hand moved to lock the door, she felt his arm brush against her waist. Her body couldn't help but react.

It had been like this all night, which was why against her better judgement, she'd said yes when he offered to show her his new place. She'd dropped a pin to Constance, of course, but still. It was very un-Bella like. Which gave her a little sense of pride when she thought about it. Provided he wasn't some crazy serial killer, it would be fine. And more importantly, it was good research. She'd realized on the car ride over that with all the talking, he'd not actually told her much about himself.

"Sorry," he murmured, looking at her as if he didn't mean it at all.

"It's fine." Brushing off the way his touch felt, she moved further into the hallway. It was a nice place, all modern fittings and wood floors. Which was about all that was in the space. The cream painted walls were bare, the polished wood doors all shut bar the lounge. She could see a simple gray couch from where she stood. She thought of her place, with the walls full of pictures of the kids. Framed copies of her book covers interspersed with awards she'd won over the years and quirky art prints she'd fallen in love with from flea markets and little art shops she'd been to on her book tours. This place was a world away from all that, and it made her wonder why he'd ever messaged her on the dating app. They were very different. "Nice place, though."

"What's wrong?" When she turned to him in question, he was right behind her. Up close, his eyes searched her face. "You have that look on your face."

"Look?"

"Yep. You've had a worried look on your face since the car." He lifted his hand, running the backs of his fingers down one cheek. "A bit like that one. What's wrong?" His hand moved till the pad of his index finger touched her forehead. "I'd like to find out what's going on in that head of yours." His brows knitted as though something had just occurred to him. "Is it about coming here?" He took a step back. "I can take you home right now if you don't feel right being here. I really did want to show you the place. Nothing else." His smile was almost bashful. "If I'm honest, I wanted the date to last a little longer."

Her rebuttal was quick. "It's not that. Being here. It's just…" She waved her hand down the hall. "We lead different lives."

"We do," he agreed, his lips quirking into a smile. "But I didn't see that when I read your profile. Now that I know more, I still don't see it as a problem. Drink?" He was already leading her toward the closed doors, his fingers having clamped loosely to hers as he slowly walked to the far door on the right. "This drink is just a drink, by the way. I didn't bring you back here to seduce you like some creep. I don't do first dates, and I definitely wouldn't end one that way, either." The kitchen was different from the rest of the house. Still bare, but real thought had been put into this room. "I make a mean cocktail, or wine?"

"Wine, please. This kitchen looks professional. Rented?"

There was a nod of his head as he took off his tie. Unbuttoning the top two buttons, she could see the deep tan that covered his muscled skin. He wasn't like the men she was used to. Not that she had much to compare him to. Gerald had pretty much been the sum total of her dating life. She'd had a couple of boyfriends in high school, but nothing worth writing home to mom about. The man pulling a bottle of wine out of the stainless steel fridge in front of her was usually the type she weaved from words. Committed to ink and paper rather than flesh and knotted muscle.

"With an option to buy."

His reply brought her back into the room and away from her idle pondering of the male specimen before her. "I wanted to put down some roots." He nodded to the stainless steel units. "The guy who owned this before me was a professional chef. Custom built this room for himself. It's one of the reasons I chose it, although it could use some modifications."

"And furniture. So, you were planning to move here? That time I saw you in the gas station?"

"No." There it was again. That little quirk of his lips, eyes that told her he wasn't showing his hand. "I decided that recently. Last week, as it goes. So, you did notice me at the gas station. I didn't think you were going to mention it."

She shrugged, blushing when she remembered her downcast mood that day. The syrup marks on her comfy clothes. "I wasn't having my best day. I'm more surprised you noticed me."

"You're pretty hard to miss." His dark eyes looked almost onyx as he fixed his gaze on her. She felt the heat between them and looked away.

"So, consulting must pay pretty well. What type of consulting do you specialize in?"

"Security. It pays the bills, but I've been thinking about winding down. It jades a person after a while."

He reached into the fridge, filling a glass tumbler with a handful of ice and grabbing a water bottle. "You're not having a drink?"

"Not much of a drinker. Besides, I'm not letting you get a

cab home. I drive on dates from now on." He rounded the island, pushing the stem of the wine glass into her waiting hand. "I couldn't wait to come off the road after riding it forever. I wanted to put down roots, make something mine, rather than living out of a suitcase." He looked around him as if he was seeing his new home for the first time. "Sure, it's a little bare. Seeing your house tonight really brought that point home, to be honest."

She blushed, covering it with a swig of her wine as he leaned against the island in front of her. "Ah, I see. You stopped travelling the world, and now you hanker for a home full of clutter like mine?"

"Life."

"What?"

"Life. Your house is full of life, not clutter. Everything in your hallway is there for a purpose. A memory. I don't think I even have one framed photo." He swallowed, his jaw clenching. So fast she almost missed it. "Not one I could display, anyway."

"Well, if you ever come to my house again, I'll remind you of your opinion. When you see the shoe marks on the baseboards, and the sweet wrappers stuffed down the couch."

"When," he smirked. "When I come to see your house, I promise not to look at the imperfections you see." He met her eyes. "Too much?"

She couldn't help but smile. "You're pushy, but I'm not running. Yet."

His grin was wolfish. "Oh, darling, I never lose something I've set my sights on. I have every intention of proving you were right to keep me around."

———

The rest of the night was pretty easy after that. He'd led her through to an equally bare lounge, where they'd sat together on the couch and he'd asked more questions about her life. He was so interested, so…receptive. Kind of annoying, too. He wasn't exactly deceptive with his answers, but he was vague about the details. She had no reason to not believe his words, but she got the sense he was holding things back. She got the sense he was a bit of a loner, focusing on work. The way he spoke about his life, her sense of who he was at his core came into focus. He was well travelled, but an observer.

Much like me, she thought when she laid under the sheets the next morning, using her snooze button to give herself a few extra minutes to process the date. He'd dropped her off outside the house, pulling up in his car and insisting she wait. Jogging around to her door, he'd walked her up the porch right to the front door. His fingers had reached for hers, banding around them as he led her up the steps.

"Thanks for a good night. I had a great time."

"The pleasure was mine. I love a good grilled cheese." He rumbled out a laugh, low and deep, and then he leaned in. She felt herself freeze, and from the way he paused, she knew it hadn't gone unnoticed. He didn't seem to miss much when it came to reading her. He stayed there, his mouth so close to hers that puckering up would be all it took for their mouths to meet.

"I'll call you tomorrow." He tilted his head, brushing his lips gently against her cheek. By the time she'd opened her eyes, he was heading down the neat, grass bordered path to his car. Stumbling to regain control of her feet, she headed inside.

"Hey," Erin had called from the lounge as Bella half ran toward the nearest window. She'd been just in time to see his knowing smirk from the driver seat before he'd given her a little wave and the car pulled away. "You didn't bail, then! Must have gone well."

"Yeah." She grinned, staring out at the dark street and picturing him driving home. "You could say that."

Her alarm sounded again, bringing her out of her daydream. He said he'd call today. She had a feeling he just might follow through. She wanted him to, but what then? Where was this going?

Ugh, you're that girl now.

Still, her rambling inner pick-me girl was definitely over-thinking things today. His place was like Superman's Fortress of Solitude. Manly and very sparsely decorated. Her place was like the before shots on one of those decluttering hoarder programs she binge-watched when the writer's block had first struck.

He knew about her kids, but he didn't know about *parenting* her kids. How dating her meant being in their lives, too. They weren't exactly the run of the mill, cookie cutter kids. She was pretty sure her eldest was already on the FBI watch list, for one thing, but hey–what was a government agency flag between dates? Evan was a full on jock, one who was angry at his father and didn't want to talk about it. And Poppy–well, Poppy was dealing, just about. She was also unique, and even at five she knew her own worth. She never shied away from putting her personality out there. Even if the PTA seemed to think she was having some kind of gender crisis.

And then, there was the extra baggage she had to bear. In the shape of flabby jowled Gerald, who would no doubt be a nightmare once he found out she was dating. And given that John was far better than Gerald, in looks and pretty much everything else, she knew her soon to be ex-husband would try to ruin it. If she thought about it in reverse, she knew she would probably run for the hills if she dated John with all that attached. She was pretty sure that before too long, he'd get bored or find someone else on the app.

The app. That was a point.

Lunging for her phone, she brought it up on the screen and searched for his profile. Nothing.

"What?" Bringing up the messages, she saw that they were still there, but his avatar was blank. Clicking on it, a message popped up. *User not found.* "He deleted his profile?" She sank back in the pillows. "Ghosted. Makes sense."

She dumped her phone on the bedspread with a huff. She really was going to fire Constance now. She'd be checking in soon to see how the date went, and she would rather fire her than have to recount her humiliation. Especially after gushing how well it had gone hours before. Maybe she could delete her messages before Constance read them. Her phone beeped before she got the chance.

Morning. I had fun last night.

She jolted upright. John had messaged her. She tamped down the rush of adrenaline that shot through her. He was a gentleman, and he was going to end it with a message. She thought for a long moment whether to bother replying at all, but decided on something neutral. Easy.

Me too, thank you.

There. Easy. Breezy. Lemon fricking squeezy. She watched the dots dance across the screen and waited for the bomb to drop.

Looking forward to date number two. I deleted my profile on the app, by the way. Might be a bit presumptuous on my part, but I am looking forward to seeing how this goes.

"No shit, you did. Gave me a dang heart attack," she mumbled, typing back.

Oh, you did? Haven't logged in recently.

Good to hear, he replied. *Have a good day. Will call you later.*

You too, she told him, before shoving a pillow over her face to stop the grin from splitting her face in half. He liked her. Enough to delete the dating app *and* tell her about it. As if he knew she'd look. Which, of course, she had, but he didn't need to know that. She didn't have to spill all her secrets.

He wanted to see her again. Her! She couldn't believe her luck, until she remembered she'd just been talking herself out of the very same thing. It could never work, not long term. She needed to keep her feet on the ground and not get swept up like one of her characters. This was reality, not fiction.

No, she'd have to just see this for what it was. Research. Very enjoyable and sexy research, but research all the same. Dating with an end date. A month, say. She'd give it a month and then pull the plug. Quicker if he followed the three-date sex rule. She was definitely not ready for that. Her waxer probably thought she'd died by now, and the way she'd flinched when she thought he was going to kiss her on the doorstep was another big reason. She just wouldn't know what to do with a man like that. John Smith looked like he could rock a woman's world, not just her headboard. She remembered the muscles on his arms, taut and corded beneath his shirt…

"Mom!"

Reality pulled her out of her daydream of powerful arms and tanned skin. She could hear little feet moving around now, just as the scent of coffee wafted up from downstairs. Thank God she'd come around from her almost kiss well enough last night to set the coffeemaker up.

Pulling up the app, she clicked a few buttons.

Profile deleted.

"Mom! Tell Daisy to get out of the bathroom! I need my gym shorts!"

"Coming," she trilled, shaking her head. Time to get on with real life again.

CHAPTER
TEN
JOHN

"Good morning, Mr. Black."

"Morning, Hannah," John replied, his voice a monotone of boredom. "To what do I owe this pleasure? Radio silence, remember?"

"Jasper asked me to call. He's had a couple of high profile jobs come in. Wants the best, and he said you're still one of us till the job's complete."

John snorted as he rose from his comfy bed. The hotel beds he was used to were usually either opulent and ostentatious or a rife fabric abode for bed bugs the size of rats. It was nice to sleep on a mattress he owned for once. "Tell him he has an agency full of the best. Some of whom I recruited for him. I'm out."

"He thinks you will reconsider."

"I won't."

"He thinks you've become jaded. Hence the domestic job you've undertaken." She paused. "He's not right, is he? The whole book order thing, returning deposits. It's a little out of character, even I can see that."

John huffed at the irritation he felt. "Hannah, my finances

are none of your or Jasper's concern. I haven't had a personality transplant overnight. It's just a job with a different planned outcome."

"But you don't usually rent property. Property implies that you are staying put."

"And I am."

"In the town you have your last target."

"I already told him, and you, this job is different. I will do it my way, on my time."

"Jasper knows you could have taken her out by now. Several times over."

"That's not the job."

"It's a hit–that is exactly what the job is. Jasper will keep at this till you tell him the truth, you know."

"Goodbye, Hannah."

"John–"

"Tell Jasper not to get involved in this. I mean it. I know where the bodies are buried. Remind him of that again before he starts looking for ways to keep me in. This is not a government or an agency job. I did my time for them, and for the agency. I am out. Now, let me enjoy my morning in peace." He looked out of his bedroom window at the people enjoying their normal lives. "The job will be done, as promised. My way. There are more pieces on the board than you know on this one."

"I know you took a job you wouldn't normally touch with a bargepole. I know you don't take jobs bumping off soccer moms. I know you really like this woman."

"Exactly." He smiled, watching a kid with a cute little backpack whirl around his dad's legs as they walked up the sidewalk together. "So, back off and let me do my thing."

He clicked off the call without waiting for a reply.

"Amateurs," he grunted, heading to the coffeemaker.

Checking his watch, he was surprised to see it was only eight in the morning. *Good,* he thought, abandoning the coffee in favor of another idea.

On his way back to the bedroom, he took in his surroundings through fresh eyes. Her eyes. The place was pretty soulless. Years of living out of a bag had done that. He'd never bothered with possessions. Tech, sure. Nice clothes? Absolutely. But nothing tangible. He'd not even noticed it before.

Pulling open his wardrobe, he selected a pair of black jeans and a powder blue button down shirt. It was time to make contact with his target again. The messages this morning had only made him want to see her face more. Especially since he knew from cloning her phone that she'd checked out his dating profile. His damn fingers had been texting her the second he'd got the notification. And a few minutes after they'd signed off, her profile had been deleted.

He was in.

Operation Belle and the Beast, as he liked to call it, was a go. He couldn't wait to build her a fricking library. He'd already bought a bookshop in the next town to cover the sales. Hannah had laughed when he'd called back to tell her his idea. The bookshop owner, deep in medical debt after her husband's stroke, was thrilled with the surprise offer. And to boot, she was a huge Bella fan, so the boatload of books showing up to stock the place had been seen as nothing but a sweetener from a very private hands-off buyer. She got to run the place, and he got to get the money from Gerald out of his account and back to his family, where it should have been in the first place. A few library shelves was nothing compared to what he would do for her. His hard, cold heart when it came to her, was as soft as a mewling kitten.

As he got changed, his phone beeped with another notification. *Bella's doorbell camera.* Bringing up the camera at the front of her house, he saw the car driving past. Gerald. He watched through the camera as the car slowed to a near halt, before picking up speed and driving out of sight.

"Checking for my car, eh, Gerry? I think Bella has a little more class with her dates than you ever did. I think you and I might have to meet, sooner than expected."

Switching apps, he brought up the tracker he'd placed on Gerry's car after dropping Bella on her date. He was heading towards his gym on Elm. No doubt to try to plug the hole in the finances until his plan came off. "A workout sounds pretty good. I've always wanted to join a gym."

BELLA

"Hey, Crista! The usual, please."

"You got it." Crista rang the order up on the register. "Muffin, too?"

Bella winced, remembering how tight her tailored trousers had been to winch over her spreading ass that morning. "Er, no. Fruit cup, please. And sugar-free syrup on the latte."

Crista winced. "That bad, huh? You know you'll need a sugar rush to get that book done." She grinned at Bella, making the tiny diamond nose stud she wore twinkle under the lighting. "How are you, anyway? You've not been coming around after the school run like you usually do."

Swiping her card, she shrugged. Half of her wanted to say that, actually, the evening staff had seen her eating the night before with a hot man, but as usual, she didn't open her mouth. Crista was one of the few people she trusted in Andersen following the scandal. "I didn't fancy feeling like a goldfish being stared at through the glass. It doesn't help with the word count."

"Well," the barista said with a kind smile, "Nice to see you back. Profits have been down thanks to your lack of caffeine intake. I'll bring it over."

Bella laughed. "Thanks. I'll be in my usual spot."

Turning away from the counter, laptop bag and oversized handbag in hand, she headed over to her usual table. Her favorite spot, in the corner at the back. Right in front of the large window that looked out onto the street. Only this time it was occupied. By a familiar handsome face.

"Oh! Hi."

He looked up from his paper, half drunk coffee, and a plate containing two of her favorite cranberry muffins in front of him on the square wooden table.

"Hello, Bella." She liked the way her name sounded on his lips. "Care to sit?"

"Oh, no, I…" He was up and out of his seat in one fluid movement, his arm coming up to lift the straps from her bags and set them down under the table. The other hand pulled back the chair opposite him. Their eyes met, and he didn't move his gaze from hers as she sank into the seat. "Well, maybe just for a minute." He resumed his seat, folding the paper and placing it on the table. "No work today?"

His lip quirked. "I'm always working."

"Right." She found the corners of her mouth lifting. "Mr. Mystery."

"Hardly. Someone told me the coffee was good," he smirked. "What brings you here today?"

Her fingers tapped on the surface of the wood between them. "Well, I wasn't getting any work done at home, so I figured I would leave the house I am sick of cleaning up and come to my old spot."

His amused gaze fell to the table after a long moment. "And you found me. Your very handsome date, sitting in your spot." The tiniest ghost of a smile made his eyes light up from within. "Some would say that was fate."

"Some would say it's stalking, too." Her joke was rewarded with a soft chuckle.

"That, too." He nodded, scooping up the paper. "I'll let you get on with work."

She could have let him go, but the second he was about to pass by her table, her hand shot out, just as her order arrived. "Don't go on my account."

Crista smiled at them both, putting the contents of her tray down and zipping off to the next customer.

"Please. I could use the company." Bella bit her lip. "I'm kind of stuck, anyway."

———

They were three coffees in, and all she'd done was open her laptop.

"So, you really don't have a plot, do you?"

"No," she laughed, even though it wasn't funny. It was actually terrifying when she thought about it. She felt the familiar tightness in her chest as she picked up the spoon sitting on her saucer. Felt the jolt when his cool hand curled over hers. They were rougher than she'd expected the first time. He had the hands of a man who had seen action, which was at odds with his polished demeanor. "It's been hard to concentrate with everything going on."

"What worries you the most?"

Wow. He knew how to read people. He always seemed to

know what she was thinking, even if he looked at her half the time as though he was trying to figure her out. She wrote about searching gazes in her books, but this man was the epitome of the definition.

"The kids, definitely. They've been through a lot, and I just want to keep the wheels turning for them. Money, I suppose, is the biggest stress. My career's a close second. I'm on my own now, and Gerry is…" She stopped herself just in time, before she spilled her guts yet again and scuppered her chances for another date. Which, having sat here for most of the morning in his company, she now realized she really wanted that date, regardless of any expiration date she'd attached to it. "Sorry. That's not your business."

"Probably not, but if something is bothering you, I would like to know. You get fidgety when you're upset, and you have a little frown line between your brows, which I can see because you're worrying." When her mouth fell open, he shrugged, drinking the rest of his coffee. "Plus, you have writer's block, which means you're too occupied with everything else to follow your passion, and that's a shame, because you are really talented."

She took a deep breath, willing her face to open up, to hide the tell-tale crease she'd seen herself in the mirror a little too many times lately. "You've read my book? You never said. Which one?" She blushed. "The latest one wasn't that well received by my core base."

"I've read anything you've ever written, Bella. I have them, actually."

His eyes felt like they were looking into her soul as he spoke. *Is it getting hot in here, or have I started hot flashing to top everything else off?*

"Always had a Bella Carmichael book with me when I travelled," he continued. "I know some people think they are just romance, but there's a lot more to them. Your characters really speak to me. I loved your last book, by the way. It was different. Showed some raw pain. Don't be ashamed of anything you do. I'm certainly not."

"Well, *that* told me." Taking a deep breath, she felt herself uncurl just a little more. "It's the writing that worries me the most. The children are doing well, considering. We're actually quite happy, but my work…I have my fans, thanks to my books." She laughed, but the bitter tinge was unmistakable. "They always thought I had this perfect life, you know. This elusive New Yorker persona that hid me enough to really push the limit on the stories I told. Life was quite easy, I suppose, if a little boring compared to my PR polish. I was married, I thought quite happily. Well, I was settled, I guess. We had three children." Her smile went wide. "Three perfect, unique kids that someday I am pretty sure will take on the world. My eldest already has, in a way, but the blowback was…uncomfortable. After the last book came out, I guess I just think that my voice is lost somehow, in all the rumors and the hurt. I don't regret the book, I guess it just proved to me that my own perspective has changed. Now, in this new chapter, I really don't feel like I have anything to write about that people would even want to read."

"Your life changed; it was bound to bleed out onto the page. Your fans love you." He said it as a statement. A bold one, with steel words. "People get betrayed all the time, even with love. Especially with love. There is no happy ever after, not for many people. I say, lean into it work wise. Show the fans your pain. Just like you did with the last one."

"Yeah, but it didn't do as well. I got new readers, but sales were down slightly. Things like that make publishers nervous."

His head cocked to one side. "If you write what you feel,

I'm pretty sure your fans will follow you anywhere. I know I would." She didn't miss the way his eyes widened, as if the last part was only meant for his head. "No one can stay the same forever. Eventually, things change. It doesn't mean life, or writing, is over."

Bella forgot to breathe for a moment. He was right. She was different. She might not write about romance so much anymore, at least not in the same way. She wasn't the same, so her writing had changed. It made so much sense. She just had to stick with her gut and her heart and see where both led her. Taking in the man before, she realized that didn't just apply to the stroke of the keys, either.

John rose to his feet, pushing the laptop lid closed. "I'm hungry. Let's get some lunch."

"Lunch?"

"Yeah." He nodded, tipping his head toward the bags at her feet before stooping to scoop them up. "I think we have time before you pick the kids up. Let's have a second date, branch out of this cafe. You never know, we might just stumble on a plot idea or two."

CHAPTER
ELEVEN
BELLA

"Mom!"

"Hey, baby! You had a good day?"

"Yeah. Mrs. Ballard said I could play table football if I finished all my maths!"

Bella groaned inwardly as she put on a happy face for her youngest. She could already see a couple of the parents turn to listen as her child barrelled into her, a baseball cap covering her long curls.

"Ooof!" She cuddled Poppy to her, taking a whiff off her shampooed hair. "Anything that gets you working is good with me, honey. Where's your brother and sister?"

"Here." Her eldest son ambled up, with a backpack slouched over one shoulder, a football under one hand, and a hockey stick in the other. He was still in his sports uniform, sweaty hair stuck up at all angles and mud on his flushed pink cheeks. For a second, his frowning features made him look so much like his father that it took her very breath away. But when she pulled him in for an awkward hug, he smiled despite himself, and then he was all hers. "Mom, do you have to?" He moaned even as he dropped the stick onto the grass to wrap his gangly arm around her.

"Aww, hush," she pretended to chide, enjoying the feel of him in her arms. God knows she didn't lean in to sniff his hair. Her nostrils were already being assaulted by the mixed scent of grass, sweat, and deodorant that emitted from him. "You could always get the school bus home, you know, if I'm such an embarrassment."

"Not a chance." He leaned down to pick up the stick in one fluid motion. "I'm starving, and this gym bag is heavy." Their sister appeared, walking over to them with her head in her tablet, headphones peeking out of her ears.

"What's for dinner?" she asked the second she set her eyes on her waiting family. Looking down at her little sister, she grinned as she pulled the speakers out of her ears. She always made time for her siblings. The protective streak she had in her was fearsome at times, but Bella could feel nothing but gratitude for it. "Nice cap, kid. Told you it would keep your hair out of the way."

Her little sister beamed up at her. "Thanks, sis. Mrs. Ballard let me wear it in class."

"Mrs. Ballard?" Daisy raised a brow at her mother. "That woman was a total nightmare when I was in her class." She stuck her tongue out at Poppy, but there was love behind the motion. "You must be her favorite, you little squirt."

"I'm everyone's favorite," she declared solemnly, which made them all laugh the entire way back to the car.

Bella loved it, all of them together. All the hats and bits the kids left under the seats, talking about coding, and the smell of sweaty jock in her messy mom mobile. It was one of the favorite parts of the day, and after spending the whole day with John, she felt rested. Energized even. Less stressed about work. She wasn't even bothered about getting home to the laundry and making dinner. Perhaps in time, she could even invite John around to meet them. Although, she would have to clean the house up before that. Organize the chaos. To her surprise, it was her kids who brought it up first.

"So," Evan said as Daisy tried to pump some emo band through the Bluetooth. Poppy moaned dramatically from the back seat next to her, begging for Taylor Swift, and the two broke out into a shrill and rather brutal sounding struggle. "How did your date go last night?"

The two girls stopped fighting, leaning in closer.

Bella slammed on the brakes as she almost missed the stop sign at the end of the street. "Date?" She tried to laugh it off, but it came out like a hyena cackle. "I went to a book club."

"Nope," Daisy piped up from the back seat. "I saw the photos on the PTA page. You weren't there. You never go there."

"I do," she refuted. Well, she had gone a few times, but it wasn't even a book club, really. Just an excuse to go to each other's houses once a month and bitch about everyone who wasn't there. Chrissie had once remarked that The Handmaid's Tale wasn't such a bad idea in theory, given the declining birth rates and lack of defined family roles. Bella hadn't been back since, and she'd gone and bought copies for the school library the very next day as an anonymous donation. Luckily, the school librarian was a fan of her books and despised the PTA since they'd tried to ban Winnie the Pooh books because, 'he didn't wear trousers and the school should not be promoting casual nudity in the arena of children's books.'

"No, you don't," Poppy chimed in, readying her hammer for the next nail in Bella's fake alibi. "You said they all bring broomsticks and stir the cauldron, remember?"

"I remember. Thanks for that, Pops." She met Daisy's eye in the rearview, and they both tried not to laugh. "Fine. I wasn't at the book club. I did have a date. What gave me away?"

"You didn't wear those gross sweatpants for once." Evan grinned. "We're not stupid. Erin kept changing the subject when we asked where you were."

"And you didn't take the car," Daisy added. "So, who is he? Do we know him?"

"No, you don't. He just moved to town, but he knows about you guys."

"Do you know his social security number?"

"No, Daisy, and no more background checks on people or you're grounded." Ignoring Daisy's frustrated growl, she turned to Evan. "Are you okay with this? I don't have to see him again, if any of you are not."

"We're okay, Mom. We don't mind Brittany, do we? Even though she's a bit annoying."

Despite the fact that she was a mature woman, Bella couldn't help but feel a ripple of satisfaction at hearing that. Brittany had been around the kids a while now, and she knew she was good with them, but the thought of another woman helping to raise her kids was a tough pill to swallow. Especially with a stepmom who was younger than some of the garments in her underwear drawer. Brittany wasn't a bad person, but being part of the reason her marriage broke down so publicly, it wasn't always easy. "Oh, Brittany's okay. She always makes the effort with you all." She looked across at Evan, but he was avoiding her gaze. It was harder for him, being the eldest. He remembered more of the times that his mom and dad had been happy. Going from that to living with a load of females, she knew he felt it pretty hard. "But she is pretty annoying." She nudged Evan, and he broke out into a smile.

"So annoying," the girls said in unison.

"It would be okay, though," Evan said long after the car fell into an easy silence. "If you had someone. As long as we can meet him."

"You want that?" Bella asked, her voice choked with emotion. "To meet John?"

"Yes," they all said at the same time, and the car descended into laughter.

————

Bella's phone rang just as she was knee deep into making tomato sauce.

"So," the deep, calm voice said, "What do you think I should get to make my place look less like a soulless black hole?"

"What?"

"It's John. I'm sitting in my empty place looking at furniture online." She turned down the easy listening playlist on the kitchen stereo and seasoned the sauce with some chopped basil. He paused. "You busy? You sound busy."

"I'm just making some sauce for dinner. Pasta night tonight." She twiddled some buttons on the oven to warm it for the garlic bread slices she was about to pull out of the freezer. "As for the furniture, don't go for something you think someone should go for." She looked around at her cozy kitchen, thinking of his stainless steel fortress. "I remember when we first moved in. I wanted to put my own stamp on the place. Your place is geared up like it was designed for efficiency. Or surgery."

"Well, I have been known to amputate the odd limb."

"Funny. I say just pick what you like, what you need." She thought about his stark living room. "A nice coffee table, a rug or two. Soften the edges a little."

She could hear his responding chuckle down the line. "One thing people never say when talking about me."

"What?" She lifted the steaming wooden spoon to her lips, taking a tentative taste. "Hmm, that's pretty good."

"Soften the edges. What's good?"

"My sauce. I hate cooking, but I do make a mean bolognese sauce."

"I'll have to try it sometime."

"What are you having for dinner?" She asked, picturing him in his empty place, laptop on his knee.

"Oh, I don't know. Takeout, probably. So, as far as furniture goes, no mass-produced bachelor pieces. Got it."

She'd seen the takeout boxes in his fridge. All stacked neatly. Looking through the door, she could hear the distant twangs of the kids on various electrical devices. She'd have to drag them out of their rooms to eat at the table, then she'd be left alone for the night while they went back to killing noobs, or in her daughter's case, taking down big pharma or something equally as frightening.

"Do you want to come here?" she asked before she could stop herself.

"I…er."

Wow, she'd actually managed to stump Mr. Cool.

"I didn't expect that. What about the kids?"

"They'll be here, too," she quipped. "It's just dinner. They don't have to know you're anything but a friend." She cleared her throat. "They did call me out on the book club thing, though, so I told them about you."

She felt the pause down the line. Maybe this was a bit too much?

"If you're sure I wouldn't be imposing, I'd love to. You want me to bring anything?"

Evan chose that moment to practise ball in the lounge, and she heard Daisy shout, "Hey, dipshit! You hit my laptop lid, you total dink! God, you're annoying!" Poppy, who was watching Wreck It Ralph for the millionth time, yelled, "Swear jar, Daisy! And shut up, I'm watching my movie, damn it!"

As a high-pitched scuffle broke out in the next room, Bella stirred the sauce with a dramatic sigh. "Maybe some wine? Ear plugs might not be the worst idea."

She heard his low, rumbling chuckle. "Half hour?"

An expensive sounding crash came from the living room, and the kids fell suspiciously silent. She heard Evan curse, and Poppy shouted, "Oooh, you're in trouble now."

"Fifteen?" she said in a desperate sounding squeak. "And maybe make that two bottles."

———

Harmony and broken ornaments had been restored and binned respectively by the time John arrived.

"Hi," he said softly, standing on the doorstep in a Henley and jeans. He looked gorgeous, like he'd just walked off a catwalk rather than the few steps from his sleek car. "I got you these."

The flowers were beautiful, bright seasonal blooms wrapped in tissue paper and topped off with a ribbon in her favorite colour, lilac.

"Wow, thank you. I'm going to need more vases if you keep this up." She took the flowers, breathing in their heady scent. She also caught a whiff of *his* scent, which was even better. She flushed as he stepped over the threshold. They were so close together in the hall, all she could smell was her date. Reminding herself she was with her kids, she went ahead to the kitchen, muttering about putting them in water, when his hand closed over her forearm, pulling her in.

"Breathe," he commanded, leaning in and kissing her cheek. She almost buckled at the knees as his stubble brushed her skin. "It's just dinner."

"Uh huh," she managed to get out. She couldn't miss his smile as he pulled back and lifted the brown bag in his other hand.

"Let's get one of these open, eh?"

"Good idea," Bella said, just as she noticed his eyes move to the lounge door. When she turned to look, Poppy was eyeing them both from the doorway. "Er, John, this is Poppy."

John put the bag by his feet, leaning down to meet her at eye level. "Hello, Poppy." He held out his hand. "Nice to meet you. Your mom invited me for dinner, if that's okay with you."

Poppy eyed his hand for a long moment before sliding out from her hiding place. She was dressed in dungarees and a checked shirt, looking more lumberjack than pre-schooler. Wreck-It Ralph was still playing from the lounge. "Do you like Disney?" she asked him, her little brows frowning atop her scrutinizing eyes. "Or Pixar?"

John, to his credit, didn't look scared at being accosted by a small child. He put a finger to his lips, tapping it against his mouth thoughtfully. "I'll be honest, Poppy. I've only ever seen one, but they both sound kind of fun. What are you watching?"

Her thumbs went into the denim of her dungarees as if that would unlock the answer. "Wreck-It Ralph. It's my favorite." Then, before Bella could utter a word, her little hand was reaching for his. "Come watch it with me. Daisy's hacking stuff on her 'puter, and Evan's talking to a giiirrll."

"Am not!" A chorus of denials rang out, and she swore she heard a tiny chuckle come from John.

"Kids, we have company!" Bella half sang, half threatened. John was already letting Poppy take him by the hand. He looked at her questioningly over his shoulder. "This okay?" he mouthed at her. She couldn't help it. She couldn't and shouldn't compare, but in her head she was replaying all the times when Gerry had come in from work and been asked by one of the kids to do something. Even before he checked out of family life, before the cheating started, he was never really there. Not really. "Bella?"

"Sorry, yes. Of course. Dinner will be on the table soon."

"You don't need a hand?" One of his hands was reaching for the bag whilst the other was dwarfing Poppy's, who was looking up at him like a big friendly giant who'd come for tea. As she shook her head, he lifted the bag till the handles brushed her fingers. "Well, make a start on this then, eh?" A little hand tugged him as he stood to his full height. "I have a movie to watch."

As she set the table, pushing the platter of garlic bread to the center, she could hear Poppy's giggles. When the rest of the food was out, she peeked around the corner of the sitting room door. John sat right in the middle of the kids. All three of them. Electronics and balls were well and truly down as four pairs of eyes stared at the screen.

"So," John said, concentrating on the screen as Poppy gazed up at him. "They all live in a video game, but when the video game gets unplugged, that's it?"

"Yeah." Daisy nodded, pretending not to be invested in the film. "But I could hack that, you know. Those old video games have such basic coding."

"Yeah," her brother snorted. "But you can't hack the power. Once the plug gets pulled, that's it. Dead. Finito. RIP, Ralph."

"No!" Poppy wailed, before bending her arm and charging at Evan's torso with a flying elbow and a murderous look on her face. "He's not dead! You are!"

Bella didn't even see John move. One second he was sitting on the couch, eyes on the screen. The next, he had lifted Poppy mid attack and was heading her way.

"Well," he said with one child tucked under his arm and the other two looking at him in awe, "I think it's time for dinner, right, Bella?"

———

Trudging down the stairs several million hours later, smelly gym holdall in hand, Bella walked into the kitchen. Poppy, high on having a visitor to quiz, had finally settled down in bed for the night. And it had only taken two bedtime stories, twenty questions, and a promise that she would buy her a toolbox for her birthday. John met her at the door, took the pile of muddy clothing out of her hands, and replaced it with a large glass of cold, crisp wine.

"Oh, you don't have to–"

He was already stuffing it into the washing machine. He strode off like some kind of cleaning warrior to the laundry room off the kitchen, leaving her to take in the sight as he stuffed the clothes into the washing machine.

And what a sight it was. It was like a different room. The debris from dinner was put away, presumably in the now humming dishwasher, whilst the sink was not only empty but clean. Shiny clean. The worktops were free from clutter, leaving the rarely seen surfaces visible and so clean she was pretty sure she could eat dinner off it. The flowers were not only in one of her best vases, but arranged with the stems cut, not just plonked into a pint pot, which Gerry had once done. John clicked a button and the washer sprang to life.

"What did you do?" she asked dumbly.

He came to join her, pouring himself a healthy glass with an easy smile. "I gave us extra time together."

"No, I mean…"

"I know what you meant." He nodded toward the door, and she found herself leading him through to the lounge. After the dinner, where the kids had scoffed the food down like they'd never seen a hot meal before, they'd all gone back to the lounge and finished watching the film with ice cream and enough cookie bites to put them all in a diabetic coma. The elder two had even seen the rest of the film out before slinking off to their rooms, which was unheard of.

"Usually, I'm knee deep in washing and cleaning right about now," she mused, sitting down on the couch. He sat next to her, so close their thighs touched. She tried not to let the surprise show on her face about how nice it was to have company. Which she ended up blurting right to him.

"It's nice for me, too." He raised his glass to hers. "Cheers to a lovely night."

She touched her glass to his, her mouth suddenly dry from the penetrating look he gave her. "And thank you for cleaning up. Dealing with the kids." She chuckled. "Being a wrestling referee. I swear, you were so fast I never saw you coming."

"Did you mean tonight or…"

She blushed. "Both, I think." She thought of the dating app, his profile compared to the man sitting next to her looking like he'd been chiseled by the Gods himself. She felt like she was back at school, all giggly and girlish. Except at school she hadn't been that girl. She'd been the one with the glasses and the pile of books ever present by her side. Which kept reminding her of the reason she was doing this in the first place. "I, er, kind of have a confession to make." She looked away and focused on the bookshelves. "I didn't join that app to find a partner." He didn't say anything for the longest time. She forced herself to look at him.

He was watching her. "Why did you join it, if not for a partner?"

"For work." She licked her lips, which felt like they'd just been freeze dried. "After the last book, and the fact that I seem to have lost the ability to write these days, my agent thought it would be a good idea. So, she kind of signed me up against my will, but the whole dating thing was never supposed to be, you know, a thing. Not really. With the divorce and everything, I didn't really think about it." She was well aware she was rambling now, and his face was so neutral she couldn't tell whether he was going to walk out, throw a fit, or laugh. "So, I just thought I needed to be honest. Since I invited you into my home and you've met my kids."

"So, you're saying that this is research material?" His tone was flat, unamused. "I'm a...job?"

Shit. She was still trying to think of what to say, how honest to be, when he started to laugh. Not just a little laugh, either. The man erupted into a belly laugh that filled the whole room. She was so shocked, all she could think was how ridiculous it sounded.

"Oh God," she said through a giggle. "It does sound bad, doesn't it? I made you sound like some kind of gigolo, and to be honest, I did write a book about an accidental gigolo that was hired by a..."

"Jilted bride," he finished for her as his laughter lulled. "I remember."

"Wait, what? You've read Heart for Hire, too? That was one of my spicier novels."

She saw the blush envelop his cheeks. "Yeah, I told you I read them. All of them." His smile grew crooked. "I'm a really big fan." He sat up, clasping her hands between his in one smooth movement. His eyes grew earnest. "It doesn't matter why you were on the app. I don't really care that you didn't tell me everything. I didn't tell you, either. I'm not a stalker, but I did know who you were before we met. I've been reading your books for years. In fact, you've travelled the world with me. I knew who you were, and I knew you had kids. I just need to know what you think of this." His thumb was doing sensual things to the back of her hand now. "Us, now. Because I don't think I'm some job anymore, even if it started out that way."

He leaned closer, his lips inches away from hers now. "And to me, beautiful Bella, you are the furthest thing from a job I have ever been." His head dipped, and his lips made contact. The softest brush of skin on skin, a barely there sensation that managed to turn her insides into gooey mush. "I don't mind being used for research. Being immortalized in the pages of one of your books?" This time, his lips skimmed her neck. A flurry of tiny, featherlike touches that made her skin rise in shiver inducing bumps. "I think it's sexy. Is that what you want me for, Bella?"

She tried to speak, but the ability to form words was ironically taken from her by the feel of him, and the smell of him that enveloped her. So, she shook her head instead. A dangerous move, because tilting her chin only served to rub her cheek against the close-cut stubble on his jaw. It made her nipples pop under her clothing, so quickly and so hard that the fabric of her bra rubbed almost painfully against them.

"A yes or no answer, Belle." He pushed, lifting a hand to

cup one, as if he knew. *Was there anything this man missed?* "Does this feel like a job?"

"No," she whispered, turning to him and running her free hand through his closely cropped hair, pulling him closer. He held back just before their lips crashed together. "Tell me what you want. Are we going to do this, for real? You and me. No pretending, no worrying about anything outside this. Us." His arms slid along her body, pulling her into his lap as if she were one of her ornamental sofa cushions. "Whatever happens, you can trust me. I will look after you and your children. There's no rush to any of this, but I want you to know that if you agree to date me, properly, nothing and no one will ever hurt any of you again. Your kids wanted to meet me, right? So, as long as we take their feelings into account, I think it could be amazing."

They'd told him as much at dinner, that they'd been curious to meet the man who'd dragged their mother away from Netflix. He'd even chuckled when Daisy asked him what his credit rating was. Evan had been the most talkative, and they'd bonded over sports, which John seemed to love as much as he did.

"It could," she breathed. "I don't just really know how to do this again." He kissed the tip of her nose, pulling her closer with one arm and cupping her chin with the other hand. His skin felt so at odds with the rest of him. They were battle scarred, worn–the rest of him was clean cut and pristine. She found herself wondering what was under his clothes. Whether the hands matched other parts of him, the parts she hadn't explored yet. "You've seen this life I have. I'm not exactly baggage free."

He pulled her closer, her legs now astride him as he ran his hand slowly up her spine.

"Perfect," he breathed, running his nose along her jawline

in such a way she felt it throughout her entire body. "I've lived from a suitcase most of my life." His grin turned wolfish. "I have plenty of strength to help you carry yours, Bella. So, I'm in. The only question left is whether you're in it with me."

"John, we've had, what, one date? Real life is a lot different than grilled cheese and one family dinner."

"Three," he grinned. "And no, I won't hold you to the three-date sex rule."

Bella's mouth went instantly dry. She could feel the hard planes of his body underneath her, which made it all the more difficult to decide whether she was relieved or wildly disappointed.

"Well, I–"

"We have all the time in the world for that. Believe me, I would like nothing better than to show you just how amazing and gorgeous I think you are. I could show you right now. If we were in my apartment, in fact, I would pick you up, carry you to the bedroom, and show every single inch of your body just how fantastic you truly are."

She felt him harden even more under her body, and it was then she realized she'd been squirming in his lap. Utterly turned on by his every word. Given that she was a wordsmith herself that had made many a woman, and a good few men, grow hot by the text produced by her tapping fingers on the keys, it was refreshing to have it done to her. Said to her, by a man she'd met just a short time ago. Through a damn app, of all things. A man who was the polar opposite of not only her ex-husband, but of every man she had ever met in real life. He was even better than the men she produced in her head and recreated on the page. He wasn't pen and ink, but flesh and blood. A man who didn't look at her messy exterior, at her children who were amazing but a lot to take on, and then run for the hills. He was the type of man who ran into a building when it was on fire, when others ran for their lives or reached for their camera phones. A man who could turn a saucy romance novelist into a steaming, desperate-for-his-touch puddle of want.

"Bella," he said, his voice husky as he moved her slightly in his lap, probably to give himself a little room to catch his own breath. "You haven't said anything in a while."

"I think I lost the power of speech. All the blood left my head."

He chuckled, and she felt it resonate from his chest through her whole body. "Is that a yes? I know I might be coming on strong, but you invited me to your home tonight. To meet your kids, and be part of your day to day. There's nothing I don't like. So, I'd like to keep doing this. Not just for research, but for you. If that's what you want."

He slowly lifted her off his lap to sit back against the sofa cushions. Leaning down over her, he planted the softest kiss on her lips before pulling back to his full height. She sat there, clothes and hair askew, lips parted and panting as he smiled down at her.

"Goodnight, Bella. Sweet dreams. Don't forget to lock up tight before you go to bed."

And he left her sitting there, thinking about what she could get Constance as a thank you present. Because she owed her big time for bringing John into her orbit. Research or not, she already knew what her answer was going to be. She was officially dating John Smith. And if anyone in Andersen Falls had a problem, they would just have to deal with it.

CHAPTER
TWELVE
GERALD

"Good morning, Mannington Consulting, Hannah speaking."

Gerald tutted at the cheery greeting. Even bloody hired killers had customer service skills. Who knew?

"Yes, it's Gerry. Again. I'm calling regarding the order I placed. I still haven't, er, received it."

"The order has been placed, sir. As we said before, there is no need to chase the order. It will be completed. Goodbye."

"No!" Gerry barked as he drove through the heavy morning traffic. "Not goodbye, I want my order delivered. Have you at least got an estimated date of arrival?"

"As I said, sir," the voice held no cheer now. Hannah's words spat out like ice chips. "Your order will be completed. Don't call again."

"Hey, lady, blow me!" he yelled, putting his foot down to overtake a slow moving chevy. The woman behind the wheel flipped him off, and he honked back as he forced his car back into the left lane. He was already late for work. Not that it mattered. He was the boss, after all. They worked for him, but his PA had already been on the phone with him three times and he'd missed a call from his divorce lawyer. Whom he'd been dodging for the last few days, waiting for his so-called order to be fulfilled.

"Sir, I won't tolerate language–"

"I wasn't talking to you, but if the shoe fits. I want my order. You tell your boss that if I don't get it soon, I am going to cancel and go elsewhere."

The pause on the line made Gerry think he might have hit a nerve.

"We do not have a refund policy, sir." Then, in a far lower tone, "We don't tolerate threats, either. Take your business elsewhere at your own peril."

Gerry almost rear-ended a food truck as he pulled a sharp left without bothering to indicate. "At my own peril? Get fucked, I can do what I want, missy. I'm paying you, I'm the boss."

He slammed on the brakes as he squealed into his private space far too fast. He was still grinning at his demand when he realized Hannah was laughing. "You're laughing? What's so damn funny?"

"You," the tinkling voice replied. "You're so funny. You placed an order. It will be done. Call here again, or order from elsewhere, and you will face the consequences. Have a good day, sir."

The line went dead, and Gerry was left alone to fume in the car.

"Goddamn it!" He ripped his phone from the holder. "Why do people keep trying to control my fricking life?" He punched the steering wheel, flinching when his phone rang. "What?" he barked down the line without checking the screen.

A cold, hard voice spoke back. "Clear your schedule for eleven o'clock. The gym on the corner of Elvington. Don't be late. It's about your order."

"Who…"

The line went dead.

Gerry's lip curled up into a smug grin. "I knew I would get what I wanted."

He strode into the car dealership like a conquering hero. Brittany wasn't in, which was becoming the norm. She was still on the payroll, but half the time she was off on some audition or another and not at reception, which was what she was still being paid for. Hence his need to hire Doris, his new PA, who was currently sitting at her desk eyeing him over her red tortoiseshell glasses.

"You're late, Mr. Carmichael."

"And?"

She made a little huffing sound at the back of her throat. "Well, your nine o'clock came and left, your ten-thirty has already confirmed, and–"

"Cancel it." He shrugged off his jacket and dropped his briefcase with a thud onto the end of her desk.

He was finally going to get what he needed to solve all his problems. He could see the media now. *Local business mogul cares for children after callous wife's disappearance.* It was going to make those damn reporters crawl for forgiveness, and all those online keyboard warrior women would laud him as a heroic single dad. He was going to meet the man who was going to deliver his golden goose.

A thought occurred to him. He was going to meet a killer, after all. Maybe he should cover himself. Be smart. "I'm going to the gym."

"But you have things to deal with here, and I–"

"Not my gym. The one on Lexington. I need a workout."

Her graying brows knitted together. "But you don't go to the–"

"I do today," he retorted. "Can't have my clients seeing

me sweating in my own gym, can I? Doesn't look good. So, cancel my morning, like I said. Sushi for lunch today, I should be back by one." He had an afterthought, rolling on the balls of his feet to face her. "Don't get it from the last place, though. That stuff tasted like an orca's arsehole."

She didn't pause her tapping of keys. "Eaten many aquatic arseholes, have we?"

He laughed, waggling a finger at her. "Good one," he admitted. "Any calls?"

"Mrs. Carmichael called this morning to remind you that you still have paperwork outstanding. Apparently, your solicitor hasn't heard from you." She cast another judgemental look his way, which he had to admit was warranted since she'd been fielding the calls for weeks now. His legal representation probably thought he had Crohn's from the amount of times he'd heard her informing them drily that he was unavailable due to being in the bathroom. Still, she was good at her job. Not much to look at, but he did need to keep his nose clean given the impending scrutiny and the unwanted attention from the local media.

He still wished his daughter hadn't sold him down the river. She was her mother's child, that one. "He, incidentally, also called this morning and has already emailed twice."

She flinched as his fist hit the table hard. Recovering fast, she made a note on the pad in her hand. "I'll tell them you're unavailable."

"Thanks," he spat back, the sarcasm coating the word like tar on a hot summer highway. "Did any of the children call?" They'd not wanted to speak to him the last couple of times. He had been pretty busy the last time they'd come for a visit, and they weren't keen on sleeping over at his mother's place. Brittany got on well with them, which was something, but

Evan's game was coming up. He normally hounded him to come watch, but he'd not even mentioned it.

Bella was behind this, he knew. Had to be. She was dripping poison in their ears, turning them all against him. She knew them better than he did. She'd been the one home most of the time, after all.

"No," Doris said, not taking her eyes off the screen. "Not since the last time you asked."

"Typical," he huffed. "It's their mother's influence, I'm telling you."

Doris levelled him with a look over her chunky glasses. "Sure, Mr. Carmichael," she said in a tone that dripped with derision. "I'm sure Mrs. Carmichael has nothing better to do with her time than ruin your life."

"You can't talk to–"

"I have things to do, appointments to cancel." She shot him a smile that didn't attempt to meet her eyes. "Enjoy your workout, boss."

Gerald made sure to slam the door on his way out. These women, they were going to be the damn death of him.

———

The gym was nothing like the gyms he owned. Carmichael gymnasiums were all glass walls and polished surfaces. Smoothie bars and protein-packed meals at the in-gym café. This place was like something from a knock-off Rocky movie. His nostrils twisted as the smell of leather and sweat hit him. With every step he took, he could feel the aroma permeating his designer suit. There was no welcoming reception desk to greet him, no gym bunny type of receptionist to sign him in. It was all barbells, heavy weights, and mats, all centered around two large boxing rings in the middle of the square warehouse.

"Hello?"

The sound of weights clanging from the back continued unabated. Muffled, as if the user was in some side room he couldn't see from his viewpoint.

"Mr. Carmichael."

The heavy statement of his name shivered up his spine as he whirled around to face the owner of the voice. A man dressed in black boxing shorts and a tight white T-shirt eyed him with a stare that made his skin sweat beneath his suit. Something about him looked a little familiar, but he couldn't place it. He looked like any man. No discerning features. Good looking, with a symmetrical face. The type of man who could disappear in a crowd.

Feeling a sudden flicker of unease, he stammered out a reply. "Er, yeah, that's me."

The man's eyes darkened, leaving Gerry to question his reply.

"I know. I wasn't asking." The man was clean cut, neat. A thin sheen of sweat gleamed on the exposed parts of his chest, but his breathing was undertaker calm. "I know exactly who you are, and why you're here. I don't like being told what to do, either."

Gerry felt his step falter, but he kept moving toward the man. Felt his chest puff out even as his insides turned to jelly. "Well, I don't like being summoned."

The man's laugh turned that jelly to water. He tilted his head in the direction behind Gerry. "Sounds like we both have issues, then. We could always discuss this in the ring."

Gerry never intended his returning chuckle to come out as a girlish giggle. He cleared his throat to cover it, gesturing to his suit. "I...er, I'm not exactly dressed for it. Armani."

The man's face was like granite, immovable and without expression. "Fine. Another time, perhaps." He folded his arms, and Gerry noticed his hands were not only huge, but wrapped and ready for gloves. "Calling the office is not an option anymore."

Gerry snorted, his head snapping back. "I wouldn't have to if your company did their job."

He noticed the man's eyes narrow as he glared at him. "Why do you still wear the ring?"

"What?" Gerry was aghast. He'd never been spoken to like this, by anyone. Well, perhaps one person, hence the reason he was in this sweatbox in the first place. "What's it got to do with you?"

Shark eyes. The man before him morphed before his eyes. Huge, white teeth, grinning eerily, eyes so black he couldn't make out the pupils no matter how hard he squinted. "Only everything. I would think a man who hired a hit on the mother of his children to save a buck wouldn't bother with the farce of wearing some remnant of their failed marriage."

Gerry answered without thinking. "It's to cover me. I can't be implicated in the death of a woman I'm fighting with but conflicted about, can I? And my customers prefer a family man, especially when it comes to buying a car." He saw the man clench his jaw, the way his biceps flexed with tension anew. He swallowed hard. "What's your name?"

"I'm nothing to you," he sneered. "Our arrangement is what counts."

"Yeah, and when is the deadline on that? I have my legal team breathing down my neck. I need this done. I have a big business deal coming up and I need everything resolved by then." He thought of the kids. "Plus, I'll need to hire a nanny."

"For the kids you don't care about other than to be used

as props, right? Something to fit in with the image you're trying to save?"

That was it. The last straw. Sure, he might be wanting to bump his wife off, but calling him a bad father? That didn't wash. "It's none of your business. You're a contractor, someone paid to get the job done on time and on budget."

"And you paid in full, right? No refunds."

When he didn't continue, Gerry started to realize his meaning. "Oh no. That's not how this works. I was told differently."

"You were told the job would be done, and I have decided otherwise." He played with one of the wraps around his knuckles, his demeanor denoting a walk in the park more than a shady meeting. "You have no business deal. You have no money. If I had completed the job, you wouldn't have had the cash to pay me. Right?"

"Well, I, er, would have to move some things around, sure, but–"

"But nothing. I know everything about you, Gerry. And I don't like any of it. The job is cancelled. Over. And you can kiss goodbye to that deposit. Save the rest for your divorce lawyer. You owe them, as well as a lot of other people. Including the family you're trying to destroy. *Your* family. It's over, Gerry. I only met with you today out of courtesy."

"What the fuck!" Gerry exploded, but something stopped him. Rather, someone stopped him. His breath was knocked out of his lungs, his back feeling like it had smashed to pieces against the hard, dusty floor. "Get off me," he gargled as wrapped fists tightened around his tie. "Hey, I pay your wages!"

For a second, the man's expression was pure murder. Then, Gerry saw it, the tiny crack that turned into a fissure of amusement.

"You pay my wages?" He squeezed a little tighter. "What the fuck do you think I am? Some two-bit car salesman you can push around?" He shook his head, a look of bemusement flitting across his tight jaw. "I really don't understand what she ever saw in you. She's worth ten of you on your best day."

Gerry went from gasping from air to swaying on his feet. The man was so close their footwear almost kissed at the toe, and he tried to slow his breathing and process what he'd just heard. What had just happened. The guy had slammed him to the floor and then shoved him back on his feet like a child did a rag doll.

"What type of man orders a fucking hit on the mother of his children? What did she do to you, exactly?"

Gerry was suddenly a babbling mess. "She…she…"

"She nothing," he spat back. His eyes were chips of dark ice. Sharp, dangerous, and cutting. "This is over. I will not be doing your bidding, now or ever. My company doesn't do refunds, either, so that money is dead to you. Like your wife," he scowled, a sneering smile on his lips. "Dead to you, not to the world. You leave her alone from now on. You release her from your sham of a marriage and pay her what you owe. I will not allow you to take her down with you." He gave Gerry one last look as if he'd just scraped him off the bottom of his boot, and then dismissed him. "You can leave now."

As he fiddled with the strap of his bound hand, Gerry shakily turned to leave. Rage and shame flooded through him in equal measure as he heard the man growl, "Sign the papers, and don't call the office again. I will find you before you hang up the phone. And next time, I won't be as nice. I'm watching you, Carmichael."

It took Gerry the drive back to the dealership to realize two things. He wasn't going to get what he wanted from the agency, and worst of all, the man knew things. About his business, and about his money issues. He almost sounded like he knew Bella.

After screaming at his bemused assistant, he hit the Internet, tapping keys until he found what he was looking for. Dialing a number, he barely waited for the answering voice to finish their welcome patter.

"Yeah," he commanded into the phone, "I need to hire someone to look into my wife. Can you put me through to your best guy for the job?"

If there was one thing Gerry liked, it was a loophole. He might not be able to call the agency, but he had a feeling that Mr. Hit Man had made contact already. He wanted to find out just how much contact he'd made.

He might not be able to knock a guy down to the mat, but there were other ways to get his way. He wasn't about to sign any paperwork unless he had no other options. He needed Bella out of the way. It was the only way his whole life wasn't going to collapse like a house of playing cards.

BELLA

"You did what?"

Bella laughed as her agent stared back at her, mouth hanging open on the screen. This Zoom call was going a lot better than recent ones. It had been a good morning, all in all. She'd used the drop-off lane for school, which meant she could drop the kids off without running the gauntlet, and had even been eager to get back home and in front of her laptop.

For once, she'd actually submitted a chapter, and Constance had read it feverishly. Bella knew she had because she'd barely hit send before she got a reply.

"I went all in, what can I say?"

"Well, I guessed something was working based on the chapter you sent. It practically set fire to my computer! Are you seeing him again?"

Bella nodded, a smile cracking her face wide open. "Yep. He just called me from the gym, actually." *Had he.* He'd sounded out of breath, and she couldn't help but picture him all sweaty and glistening. He'd been going every day, and he always called her when his workout was done. Checking in. His voice had been deeper than usual, like his testosterone levels had been amped up by the physical exertion. He'd practically demanded to see her that night, but she'd had to tell him she couldn't because she was a mom taxi for the evening. He'd asked about the game, where it was. "He was a bit strange on the phone, though. He asked if Gerry went to the games."

Constance pulled a face like she always did these days when Gerry was mentioned. "As if. He never bothered half the time when you were together. Even when he did turn up, you said he spent half the time on the phone."

"Preach." Bella clicked her fingers together in unison. "I told him that, and how Evan kept trying to involve him. Well, the watered down version. He seems unaware of it all." She bit her lip. "You know, the colossal shitshow that was my public break-up. I've told him the details, but I don't think he realizes just how bad it got. I kind of want to leave that. It's not like I want him googling that stuff. Daisy did her thing, anyway, deleting things."

Constance chuckled. "I swear, if you ever want to tell her life story when she's older and running the White House, I want agent first dibs." She paused. "So, he's a big fan. Do you really think he's not seen some of that stuff?"

"I don't think he cares either way, he's so laid back." She thought of how John had reacted when she'd told him her story. He didn't seem overly shocked, or aware. It wasn't like the man was the type to listen to gossip rags.

He might just be the perfect guy.

"He's been travelling a lot. Not much stateside time, which is a bit of a blessing. He's different. The total opposite of Gerry. It's been…nice." Nice was an understatement. Seeing how he listened and treated her, she felt safe around him like she never had before. He was so good with the kids, and any man dating a woman with three children who demanded to meet him would have thought twice. With John, she got the impression that nothing fazed him. He was there, ready to take it all on. She thought of his strong arms, pulling her in close on the sofa. The heat between them. This was not some experiment anymore. It was…something else. "More than nice, actually. I just…" She sighed, reaching for her coffee mug but realizing she'd already drained it. "I know that this was supposed to be research, and I told him the same–"

"You told him you were dating him for research? Bella, you didn't!"

"Calm down," she laughed. "I felt bad, you know. Plus, these things have a way of coming back to bite you in the ass. I didn't want any secrets. I feel like I just spent fifteen years shrouded in them. He saw the funny side and…"

"This isn't just research anymore." Constance's reply was a statement rather than a question, and Bella nodded at her friend through the screen. "You really like him, don't you?"

Bella didn't even try to stop the grin from escaping. "Yeah, I do. He's handsome and charming. He's like one of those old school guys, you know? All about opening the car doors and protecting your honour kind of stuff. And you should see him when he came here for dinner. I swear, my kids were hosting a cross between a roast session and a smackdown, and he just walked into the lion's den without a second thought." She thought of John, sitting on the sofa surrounded by her very unique children. "He charmed them all, to be fair. Even Daisy. And he talked sports with Evan." She was gushing now, warming to her theme. "And I know I shouldn't compare, and I'm not really, but he's just the opposite of Gerry in every way. In fact, the more time I spend with John, the more stupid I feel for wasting so much time."

"Gerry wasn't always like that, though," Constance reminded her. "Give yourself some credit. You make half the women in America fall in love with your book boyfriends. You have a good eye for what works in a man, but when you've been with someone so long, it's different." She started to laugh, that tinkly laugh that Bella knew was her real one. She had another, deeper laugh too, that she usually brought out at literary events when she was laughing at a joke made by some publisher or another. Constance was a gorgeous six-foot blonde who commanded any room she walked into, but in the sometimes very masculine book industry, editors and other agents alike often mistook her outward looks for lack of intelligence. Constance read Chekhov like they were coffee time reads, did the New York Times Crossword every day of the week like Poppy did wordsearches, and could size up a douchebag from a hundred feet away. She could smell misogyny as keenly as a shark did blood in the water. These and many other reasons were why Bella and she were now much more than agent and writer—they were friends.

Which was a good thing, because over the years, living in suburbia and working from home, her friends had fallen away. Some of the moms at school were nice, but as the kids got older, the playdates lessened as they returned to work, and Bella found she didn't have much to talk about with them. Her world had gotten smaller without her even realizing it, and now that everyone knew Gerry had stepped out on her, she was not entirely happy her orbit was so tiny. Maybe now, with John in her life, she could start to look forward to the future again.

"B, you're getting in your head again. Earth to Bella!"

"I know, I know," Bella agreed, pulling her head back in the game. "You're right. I mean, those early books were all about him, really. Little pieces of Gerry woven into the characters." She shrugged, remembering the battle she was now locked in with him. "It's crazy how people change. I still can't believe he's still with Brittany. Not that I care, but I just don't get the two of them together."

Constance made a clucking sound at the back of her throat. "Oh, I do. He's the white whale to young girls like that. She went from working as a PA to having the keys to someone else's kingdom." Her shoulders rose before she looked Bella in the eye again. "Some women build their own lives and empires; other women just take them."

"She can try," Bella fumed. "She can have Gerry and his businesses. His future kids, if she wants. I just want what's mine for the kids. Honestly, you should see the paperwork from his solicitors. He's trying to make out like I just sat at home and wrote some silly stories eating Ding-Dongs and binging daytime TV while he worked like a Roman." She heard the tinge of anger coating her words. "I earned six figures last year in royalties, but just because it's not akin to his business—which, by the way, I invested in and helped grow in the early days—he just treats it like pocket change." She pointed a finger into the air. "Well, not exactly chump change. While also sneering that I did nothing and had nothing to do with his business or its success, he also thinks that I should just sign the papers and want no settlement for the kids. The way he sees it, I can keep the proceeds of the house I own half of and that's enough. But this place is worth so much more than we paid for it, and I'll never be able to buy something around here for the same amount. Not on my own. The mortgage people balk at self-employed income. And I love this house, even with the memories. The kids need to stay in the house they were born in. He just wants to pocket the profit the sale would bring and run off into the sunset. Honestly, he pays half the mortgage, but I have to beg for it. Nothing for the kids. He's an utter shit, and his lawyer is as slippery as a snake oil salesman. The cheating is irrelevant, apparently, since–" Bella air quoted in a frenzy, "–he could sue for emotional distress due to the fact that *our* daughter outed him as a cheater online. If it wasn't for Daisy, I would nail him to the wall, but with book sales dropping and the stress, you know…I just can't drain my finances fighting it. He could really go after Daisy, and I won't have that."

Constance was understanding, but Bella still saw her little smirk.

"What?"

Her agent giggled. "I know you're going through it, but damn, I love Daisy. They say the new generation is going to save the world, and she will probably be their leader. I mean, who hacks their dad, finds out they cheated, and puts him on blast? I mean, for real. I know it was a shitshow for you, but I'm telling you, if that girl ever fancies writing like her mama, tell her to hit me up. She could have a whole YA detective series under her belt by the time she graduates. I would sell the shit out of that."

Bella was still laughing long after the Zoom call ended. It *was* a shitshow, and she was still getting looks around town. People made comments. Gerry was still incensed about the perceived betrayal.

But it had changed her life. Broke her out of the rut she was just hoping to push through. It brought her back to life, and now she had a chapter she was proud of, and a man on her horizon who excited the heck out of her. More than even Gerry had in his younger days.

Picking up her phone and stepping away from her computer to get more coffee, she brought up John's number.

Hey, she typed.

Hey, beautiful. He typed back almost immediately.

What are you up to?

Just checking on a client. You okay? Bet you're already on your third coffee by now.

I'm good, and yes, stalker, just pouring my third cup. But in my defence, Poppy woke me at five-thirty to tell me she would rather die than wear the cute outfit I laid out for her. I needed the caffeine. Constance loves my new chapter.

Of course she does, you're brilliant. Don't worry about Poppy. She knows her own mind. Not every girl likes pink. Wish Evan good luck for the game from me.

She had to stop herself from hugging the phone to her chest. He was so damn cute. She was grinning out of the kitchen window like a damn idiot. If the mailman came past right now, he'd probably think she was having a stroke.

Come to the game, she typed. *Tell him yourself. We can go get pizza after, if you want to join us.*

You sure the kids won't mind?

She didn't tell him Evan had already mentioned it in the car. He'd done it in a nonchalant, typical Evan type of way, but it had struck her that maybe having someone else cheering him on in the stands might be a good idea. They were officially dating now, and Andersen Falls being the place it was, people would talk sooner or later, anyway. It might be better to get out in front of it.

I'll ask them at pick-up, but I think you've charmed them already. If you want to come, you're welcome. No worries if you think it's too much.

No, I'd love to come see him play. It's a deal. Go Panthers.

Go Panthers, she typed back. *Come to my place for, say, six?*

Can't wait, gorgeous. See you in your next chapter.

This time she did give in, doing a little twirl on the spot as she pressed her phone to her chest like a lovesick teenager. The coffee in her hand sloshed over the side, splattering the tiles. "Shit," she laughed, going to get the mop.

———

JOHN

Through his lens, John smiled as he watched Bella mopping through the window. She looked happy, he thought with a pang.

For the first time in his surveillance career, he felt like he was a Peeping Tom. He'd seen a lot of things over the years. That one senator who liked to be fed baby food by a stripper with a large spoon while he wore a nappy. He'd seen coke-fuelled orgies featuring statesmen and sex workers. He'd even seen a few tortures over the years, before his team could extract. Nothing had made him feel as uncomfortable at the other end of a lens as this did.

But it was for her own good, he knew. He'd warned Gerry off, but his office was already sensing rumblings. He'd met with a PI, and they didn't mess around. He couldn't afford for Gerry to find out how he was involved.

He'd made the mistake of voicing his opinion in front of the man at the gym, and that wasn't like John. He was never sloppy. He should have covered his face, but when it came time to arrange the meeting, he didn't want to hide behind a mask. He wanted to look the man straight in the eye.

What did she ever see in you? It had rolled right off his tongue. His incredulity was evident while meeting the man who had managed to get Bella to walk down the aisle, to have his children. Children who were seemingly nothing like him. There was no spectre of him in their lives, either, as far as he could tell. Every woman moved on from her marriage and made her home her own, but to his trained eye, the home she was bringing her children up in seemed to flow directly from her. It started and ended with Bella.

She was still swirling around the kitchen when his eyes were drawn to a black sedan pulling up to the house a few doors down, on the other side of the street. His lens moved to focus on the occupant. He saw a rather craggy-faced man John would put in his fifties. Pale, with paunchy skin and a crumpled beige jacket like something Columbo would wear on laundry day. He was messing with something in the passenger seat, out of John's line of sight.

Checking that Bella was still in the kitchen doing her thing, he reached for his gun. He checked that the silencer was on and the chamber loaded. If he had to take this guy out right on her street, so be it. It would be messier than he liked, but–

He'd wound his window down, perching a zoom lens on the glass and focusing. Right on Bella's house.

Fuck. The PI.

The little shit, Gerry, had ignored him and instructed this bargain basement detective to monitor her. He was looking for dirt. John's careless comment had somehow penetrated the weak gray matter between Gerry's ears.

He had to shut this down, and fast. The kids would be back soon, and he didn't want them to see anything. Pulling out his phone, he dialled Hannah.

"It's me. I have a PI on the target's street, a black sedan." He read off the registration number. "No, no threat. Neutralize peacefully."

"Call to PD, a concerned neighbor reporting a peeper?"

"Action it now," John confirmed. "Add the detail of the camera, too. We might need to dispose of that footage."

"Of the target?"

John's lips pursed at the wording. It sounded wrong, even though he'd just used it himself. "Target is now the client, for future reference. This is now a monitoring and security assignment only. If Jasper sees it, he sees it."

Hannah didn't miss a beat. "The file will be updated. Call is going in now."

John ended the conversation, his eyes never leaving the man who was now sitting in his car with a breakfast bagel in his hand. "Amateur," he cursed. A neighbor could easily make him. Hell, Bella only had to look out the window and she'd see the guy herself.

From his viewpoint, in his nondescript hire car, John was hidden. This guy might as well have a sign hanging on his car. "It's Surveillance 101, dickweed."

Bella was gone from the kitchen window. He scanned the other front windows. Nothing. She didn't mention going out, but she could be getting ready to run an errand. He needed this to go down without her being tipped off. "Where are you, darling? Man, I should have just taken the guy out."

Hey, what time does the game finish? He typed it in their message stream. It was a lame thing to ask, but contact was contact.

Minutes passed by, but he received nothing back. Hannah notified him when the PD was en route. The PI was on the phone now, presumably checking in. With that, John scowled and called Hannah again. "We need to double check who else Gerry has contacted. This PI is just the tip, I think. We can't afford any mess-ups."

"Slippery customer," Hannah noted, the irritation clear in her voice. "He was a real sweetheart on the phone. I'm on it." After a beat, she added, "Kind of nice to see the other side of the job." John smiled, but he didn't answer.

"Protection doesn't pay as well," he quipped. "But there are certain other benefits."

His phone pinged. *Usually around nine. That okay?*

Perfect, he confirmed. *You should be writing.*

A squad car turned onto the street, pulling up behind the PI. "Contact made," he told Hannah before pulling out on the street and driving in the opposite direction. "Pull the police report, and make sure the client doesn't get wind of it."

"No problem. I used the concerned passerby angle. It shouldn't blow back. If he's a half decent PI, he won't say why he's there. If he does, we'll manage it." She paused. "You could have just taken him out. Bella would never have known he was there."

"I thought about it. This way's cleaner."

"Understood. I'll be in touch."

Later, when he was getting ready to meet Bella, the copy of the report came through. Thankfully, they didn't have to manage a thing. The police officer had let him go, not bothering to delve further. The PI had told him he was a portrait photographer who'd gotten lost looking for a client's address and had pulled over to check the directions. Baltimore's finest had let him go after checking his file. It turned out the guy was a photographer, had only been a PI a few months, and mostly photographed cheating spouses.

The guy was nothing. A small fry, and Hannah was going to see to it that he wouldn't be working with Gerald again. As luck would have it, the IRS were very interested in the man's tax situation. The offices of one Roland Garvey wouldn't be taking on clients any time soon.

A good clean day's work, all in all. Semi-retirement was fun, and John had a hot date with the woman of his dreams. As long as Gerald let things drop, things would be fine.

As he drove over to Bella's house, he was in a good mood. Everything was coming together, and the cherry on the top would be Gerry's face when he finally realized that he had lost this battle. Bella and the kids would be safe from him, once and for all. John would make sure they were, if it was the last thing he ever did.

The school stadium was buzzing when they arrived. Andersen Falls was a big football town, and it seemed like the whole town had turned up to show their support. "Bye," Evan shouted over his shoulder as he spotted a couple of his teammates. "Don't embarrass me!"

John raised a brow at Bella, who blushed a delicious shade of pink. She was wearing a Panthers shirt and jeans, looking every inch the proud mom.

"I don't know what he's talking about," she shrugged, just as Poppy laughed.

"Mommy cries at games," she declared, smoothing down her own little team jersey over her teeny body. Her soft curls were tucked up under the ball cap she wore. "Evan says she has to stop or go sit in the car with the other weirdos."

Weirdos in cars, he thought to himself. *Must be the order of the day.*

"Yes, thanks Poppy." She flushed further until it spread to her collarbone. John could make it out under the skin exposed by her V-neck shirt. She did look a little on edge, though her make-up and hair were perfect. "Our seats are over here."

Once they were seated, the girls plugged into their own devices and headphones while the team limbered up, he turned to her and leaned in close. "You look nice." He allowed his eyes to roam, to track the pink hue as low as it went. "Do you always dress up for games like this, or do you have a hot date?"

"Thank you," she deflected, but he didn't miss the little smile that appeared. "It's more armor than anything." Her eyes darted around. "Some of these bitches smell blood in the water if you look less than perfect mid divorce. Let's just say I had a bit of a run in with the PTA women, and I'm not keen on repeating it any time soon."

"Right." He cast his own gaze around. She wasn't wrong. A few pairs of feline-like eyes were definitely observing them. He leaned in a little closer, snaking his arm out to rest around her waist. "Armor it is, then."

She blanched. He felt her back stiffen. "Oh God, I just realized how that came out. I didn't invite you for that reason. I–"

"Oh, I'm flattered that you think I'm a good protector." He squeezed her waist, just a little. Reassurance, he told himself, but also because his fingers twitched to be closer. It was becoming a bit of a problem. Especially since the one thing he needed to be was close. He still didn't know if she wanted this as much as he did. Given that the last man she was with broke her trust, it made his situation ironic, to say the least. "I thought women were supposed to stick together with these sorts of things."

Her laugh caught in his ears, and he wanted to keep it forever.

"John," she said, throwing him one of her coy little smiles, "this is the suburbs. The coyotes in the woods near here cower at the housewives when they cross paths. The only thing these women don't do is eat their young." A woman swatting at one of the team members' faces with a wet wipe and a determined scowl caught her eye. "Well, not in the way nature's creatures normally would, anyway. Here, I guess they just use them as trophies or to score points off other mothers. I swear, last season when Evan scored the most points for the team, I thought I was going to have to hire a bodyguard to swat off the dagger looks and scrutinizing stares."

Her eyes fell on Poppy. "They know what they do. 'It takes a village' is not a life lesson they ever listened to. Once they spot weakness, the rattlesnakes start hissing." As if swatting away some invisible threat, she bent to straighten Poppy's hat. A chunk of hair fell loose, and she smiled, pushing it back under the cap before Poppy's little fingers had a chance to reach out and do the same. When she saw him watching her, she straightened up. "Anyway."

She shut the conversation down with a single word, and John knew that it had presented him with more questions than answers. But he would find them out. No truth could hide from the man who cloaked himself in deceit on a daily basis.

He brushed the caress of guilt off like a stray piece of lint from his jacket. Telling himself this was his last job, he was out of the game. That he could still be a worthy man even with his past. That he told the truth to the woman in front of him, as much as he was able. He was just a master of omission to boot. He knew he didn't deserve her, that any relationship they started would be based on a lie. But being here, with her and her children, he had never felt more settled. This was the life he wanted, and he would do just about anything to protect it. To be the one to wipe that uneasy smile off his woman's face. Chase away the shadows and protect her from her enemies. She sank closer to his side, and he relished the chance to draw her in closer.

"Anyway," he said back, dipping down to brush his lips against her cheek. "Let them talk. We're all here for Evan." Pulling back, he saw a couple of the coven watching, their eyes wide. Tucking Bella closer to his side, he shot them a relaxed grin. One that looked friendly on the surface but had an undertone of 'what the fuck you looking at?' underneath. Their heads dipped, and not for the first time, John felt the protective shield he'd built around Bella bloom into something warm.

She needed him to save her, but not in every way. She had been doing a pretty job of that all by herself, but every girl needed a wolf to walk through the forest with. Someone to face the snarling beasts with. He was the Beast to her Belle. It was ironic that the only Disney film he'd ever watched in the children's home had been that one. It had stuck with him over the years, and now he was living it. Turning into a prince as she broke the curse that had been his existence before that day at the gas station. Right out of one of her novels, he would be the guy who really saw her. What she needed and wanted, without her even asking. Not only would he be that, but he wouldn't have to break a sweat doing it. The shield was natural around her, brighter and stronger than it had ever been before.

———

It was half time when Bella's phone rang. John knew who the caller was without having to look or ask. He could tell from the way her body tensed, the way her fingers gripped the phone with white fingertips. "I'll just be a minute. Could you watch the–"

"The girls are good here," he soothed, flashing them both a smile as they tucked into hot dogs from the stand nearby. "Right, ladies?"

Poppy's face scrunched up. "I'm not a girl. I'm a tomboy."

"Noted," John said, not missing a beat. "We'll be fine." The phone was still ringing in her hand, and he saw her stab the screen as she walked away from them. A few seconds later, she was looking around like a damn meerkat, her eyes roving the stalls and stands around her. "How do you know it was up to me. Evan knows his own…" He caught that much before she turned her back to him, but he pretended not to be straining to hear her and turned his attention back to his charges. Poppy was looking up at him, a smear of ketchup on her top lip.

"I think it's Daddy calling. She always acts like that when Daddy calls."

John reached for one of the spare napkins, offering it to her. "I think you might be right, sauce face." She giggled, flashing him a peek of teeth and half chewed hot dog before wiping the napkin across her lips.

"I wish he would leave her alone," her older sister said. She'd polished off her hot dog and was currently ripping a napkin into tiny pieces on her lap. "It makes her sad."

John said nothing. He didn't like the piece of shit, but a father was a father. You only got one. Having never known his own, he wasn't about to influence anyone about theirs. No matter how much he wanted to wipe the man off the face of the earth.

"Yeah," Poppy said. "And his girlfriend is so stupid, too." She looked up at him with wide eyes. "She likes pink on everything she wears, and when I told her about my science project for school, she thought Pluto was a dog."

Her big sister chipped in, "And she giggled when Pops said Uranus." Her young eyes slid back to her mother. "I kind of think I did the wrong thing when I made that post, but I really wanted to show my dad what he did was wrong. Mom said we should always tell the truth, and bad people should get what they deserve." She bit her lip. "I think he deserved it, but now he takes it out on Mom."

John's chest was hurting. Actually physically hurting. As if he had heartburn or something. He swallowed to loosen the lick of flame coursing through him. "This is none of my business," he said softly, "but I have your Mom's back, you know." Both girls were staring up at him. "All of your backs, if you want."

The eldest said nothing for a second, her eyes a little watery, before she pursed her lips and gave him the tiniest of nods. Poppy held her chin in one hand, seemingly deep in thought. Bella had hung up and started to make her way back over to them.

"Does that mean we'll get hot dogs at every game? Mom always said they spoil dinner, but she said yes because you asked."

John released the breath he'd been holding with a chuckle. "Sure."

Poppy beamed, holding out a fist. John bumped it back.

"Deal," she said, as solemnly as a warrior would take a blood oath. He was just turning to check for Bella, when Poppy added, "John?"

"Yeah?" He looked down at the mini Bella sitting next to him, her short legs swinging freely from her seat.

"We've got your back, too."

There it was again. This time, it felt like a fireball through his sternum. "Thanks, Poppy. That's worth all the hot dogs in the world."

From behind him, Bella's voice sounded amused. "What did I miss?"

CHAPTER
FOURTEEN
BELLA

"I kicked ass! Did you see, Mom? Did you see?"

"Hey!" Poppy piped up as they entered the pizza place en masse. "Dollar in the swear jar, Evan!"

Evan rolled his eyes, his cheeks flushed from the success and exertion of the game. "Ass isn't a swear word, Pops. It's an animal, like a donkey."

"Technicality," Poppy said, in that cute way she did when she learned new words but not quite in the right way. It came out like *technitality*. "You didn't kick an animal, so pay up."

John chuckled beside Bella, and she felt the familiar warmth spread over her. She felt it so much lately she'd begun to worry about menopause. But since it only occurred around him, she guessed it was less about her ovaries and more about her heart.

And about your vagina, her inner saucy minx added. Which made her blush all the more violent.

He took his jacket off as they waited to be seated, rolling his sleeves up to show corded, thick forearms. He rubbed her between the shoulder blades. "Warm?" he asked. "Give me your jacket, I'll carry it."

She was already carrying the mom crap she'd brought the game–her snack bag and handbag. She'd refused to let him carry them for some reason. Well, she knew exactly why. He'd done a lot lately for her, and she'd done nothing for him. She felt like carrying her own bags might right the balance a little.

His pursed lips at her refusal told her otherwise. That was just John, always the nice guy. Doing what she needed without being asked. Half the time before she even realized she'd needed it. She went to put her bags down as the server approached. By the time she'd pulled her jacket off, the bags were in his hands. He gave her a knowing smirk, tugging the jacket from her grasp and striding after the server who led them to a booth in the back.

The kids slid into the booth, with Poppy wanting to sit close to John as always. At the side of the booth, Bella came to a stop, and she felt John's thighs touch against hers. He didn't back away as he lowered the bags and jackets down at his feet. The kids all reached for the menus while continuing their usual hubbub of bickering and cries of starvation as they discussed what they were going to eat.

"So," John said, his voice low. "I've been kind of wanting to ask you something. I know the kids are going to see their dad this weekend."

Bella's heart dropped at the thought. Gerald had called to demand them, more like. She'd asked the kids after the game, and they'd all agreed they would go, but she could see that the older kids were not that thrilled about going. Brittany was nice to them, of course, but Gerry had them so seldomly that Bella knew it would make for an awkward weekend.

"Belle? Come back."

She pushed the thought away, flashing him a grin. "Sorry. You were saying?"

"I was saying that since you have the weekend to yourself, maybe we could do something. If you're not working."

"Mom, can we get dough balls?"

"Sure," she told Evan, then turned back to John. "I was going to work, but we could do something." She was definitely going to work. In fact, pre John, she would have spent the weekend holed up in the house in her PJs, ordering take-out and drinking too much wine. With the writer's block gone, she would have had the laptop glued to her, tapping away like a crazy person with the looming presence of her excited agent hanging over her like a shadow. It was kind of nice to think this weekend might actually be something good. Different. "What did you have in mind?"

The server was on her way over, notepad in hand. "Well," John said, "I thought I'd pick you up Saturday morning." He was leaning in close, now. "And then we'd go from there? I have a few ideas."

She found herself smiling just as the server asked if they were ready to order. "Sounds good," she told him.

He nodded, a sly little smile crossing his face. "Good," he nodded. "Pack an overnight bag." When her jaw dropped, his smile grew wider. Smooth as anything, he lifted his head and turned his attention to the kids. "Hey," he said politely to the server, as Bella's whole body burst into flames beside him. "I think we'll start with the garlic dough balls and the jalapeno poppers. What do you say, gang?"

———

When Saturday rolled around, Gerry was on time, which was the first surprise of the morning.

"Hey," she said, opening the door to him. "Kids, your

dad's here!" She could hear them upstairs, shuffling about. No doubt packing half their rooms to take with them.

After the pizza last night, she'd said goodbye to John and headed home to get straightened up. It had taken her a while to wrangle them all to bed after their sugar rush. John was a soft touch around them, she noticed. One bat of Poppy's lashes and he'd agreed to puddings before she could even think of saying no.

This morning, she'd been up with the darn lark, alternating between trying to pack her overnight bag, pack up the kids' clothes for the weekend, and cleaning. She told herself she wanted to leave it all done so she wouldn't have a lot to do on Sunday, but she knew it had more to do with Gerry. She didn't want him tattling to his legal team about a stray dust bunny or unwashed window. When he lived here, he didn't lift a finger in the way of housework, and any DIY jobs were done by paid professionals. Ones that Bella would have to find, hire, and oversee. Even then, he would moan about the cost, when he probably could have done some of it himself. He'd gone so far as to have her hire someone to install the baseball hoop in the back garden. Even the handyman was surprised when he'd knocked on the door that weekend to see a full-grown man, still in his silk dressing gown, answer the door.

Gerald looked her up and down, and she clocked the surprise on his face. *Yeah, Gerry, no sweatpants today.* She knew she looked good, and it wasn't for the love rat standing on her doorstep.

"So, what are you up to this weekend while I'm babysitting?"

How she managed to keep her face neutral, she'd never know. "It's not called babysitting when they are your babies, Gerry."

He shrugged, and she caught the little snarl on his lips. *How did I spend so much time with this man?* "Whatever. No plans, then. What a shock."

She could hear the kids coming down the stairs. "I have plans, thank you. Nothing you need to know about, just remember that. And also, Poppy picked her own clothes, okay? Don't give her a hard time about it."

He rolled his eyes. "I do know my own kids, Bella."

She didn't bother telling him the oh-so-many ways he didn't actually know about his progeny. It would take the weekend up. John would be on his way, and she didn't want to run the risk of them crossing paths. She knew he'd find out, anyway. It wasn't like she'd coached the kids not to tell him about John. She wouldn't play the games he seemingly had before their marriage ended. She still remembered Poppy mentioning Daddy's special friend at work, and not putting two and two together.

"Sure you do." She smiled back in a way that showed she didn't agree with him and that he could actually go screw himself.

His sneer widened, making her lips twitch with mirth.

She'd hit home. *Childish, but worth it.*

He was still sneering when the kids descended en masse, and before she knew it, she was waving them off. If she thought the kids wouldn't have seen, she would have flipped him off for good measure, but she waited to close the door before gesturing wildly.

"God," she growled, turning to the mirror. "What the hell were you on all those years, Bella? I mean, Jesus Christ!" He always got under her skin. She was so wound up, she let out a frustrated scream.

A knock on the door sounded half a second later, and John's concerned voice boomed out, "Bella, you okay? I'm coming in!" He burst through the door, tucking his hand back in his jacket when he saw her standing there looking surprised. "Bella?" He scanned her body as if looking for injuries. "What's wrong?" His eyes darkened. "Was it Gerry?"

She was red in the face, both from the wild swearing and hand gestures and the sight of him coming bounding through her threshold like some kind of modern-day warrior. "Er, yeah," she said as he stepped forward and tucked her into him in one swift move. "I swear, if I never saw him again, it would be heaven."

"You and me both," he muttered into her hair.

"What?"

"Doesn't matter." He nuzzled along her jaw before pulling back and dropping a kiss onto her lips. "What did he do?"

"Nothing. The usual, you know. We can't be in the same vicinity without him setting me off."

"Are the kids okay? With him, I mean."

She grinned as he tucked her into his chest. *This man. She owed the dating app Gods a sacrifice or something.* "Yeah, he's not the best dad in the world, but they'll be fine with him and Brittany. Well, Brittany and his staff. Gerry usually gets bored after a couple of hours and slinks off to work. They'll be fine. They have their phones."

"Good," he soothed, rubbing small circles along her back. "So, are you ready to get out of here?"

"Definitely." She grinned as he took her hand in his. "I put my bags in the lounge," she told him, heading to collect them. When she came back into the hallway, he was frowning at the security alarm panel on the front door. "What's up?"

He pointed a finger, his brows knitted together in a sexy,

pensive way. "When did you get this installed? The spec's not great."

"Spec? That a sensor or something?"

He turned to her with an aghast look till he saw her face. "Ha. Funny. Specifications. Mock the security geek."

"I didn't know you were a geek," she laughed as she pulled her jacket on and grabbed her keys from the dish on the hallway side table. "Very Clark Kent of you." He shot her an amused look, frowning again when he returned to the panel. "We've had it for a while, to answer your question. I barely use it. Gerry did a deal with some security firm a few years ago."

He was peering at it like a kid would an ant under a microscope. "Right," he muttered. "I have a guy who could update it for you. He owes me a favor."

She was about to tell him she didn't need it, but he was already pulling out his phone and tapping away. "Spare key?"

"Huh?"

He reached for her bags, nodding toward the front door. "Spare key. I have a lock box in the car, and we can leave it in the backyard. It'll be done when you get back on Sunday."

"John, I can't afford–"

"No charge, I told you. It's covered." He reached for her hand again, glaring one more time at the control panel. His phone chimed, and when he checked it, the frown deepened. "Time to go."

"Okay, well thanks–hey, what's the hurry?" He was guiding her so fast down her front steps, she felt like a celebrity after someone yelled that there was a security breach. She was in the passenger seat with her bags in the back before she got a chance to blink.

He slid into the driver's seat, his gaze on every mirror.

"John? Everything okay?"

He pulled out so fast he almost drove straight into the mailman, who jumped behind his cart. A flurry of letters fluttered to the ground around him like confetti.

"John! You nearly sideswiped Roy!"

"Hmm." He was still looking in his rearview, but he took his foot off the gas. "Oh, sorry. I just don't want to hit traffic. Put your belt on."

Bella glanced backward, but she couldn't see Roy for a black SUV that was on the road behind them.

She felt John's hand cover hers, bringing her attention back.

"What?"

"Put your belt on, honey," he repeated. She could swear she saw his shoulders relax a little once she'd clicked her belt into place. "Good girl."

He weaved through the Saturday traffic, turning onto a side street. Then another side street.

"Where are we going?"

His eyes were fixed on the rearview mirror, and when she turned to look, he gripped her hand tighter. "Do me a favor. Reach down into the glove box and find me a map?"

She heard a sharp clinking sound followed by the smash of glass the second she lowered her head. "What the hell was that?" She tried to put her head up, but John's arm was firm across her back.

"A stone. It hit the back windshield. Keep looking for the map," he commanded, gripping her arm just as he turned a sharp corner.

Cars honked their horns all around them, and she could hear the noises of the freeway getting louder. "John, what's going on?"

He didn't speak, his foot on the gas as he hit the on ramp at speed. She bounced around in the passenger seat, managing to locate a folded map right at the back of the compartment. "I got it!"

This time when she lifted her head, he didn't stop her.

"What the hell was that?" They were on the freeway now, zipping up the fast lane. "Don't you have sat nav?" She could hear the wind whistling, and when she turned to look, she saw why.

"They must have been resurfacing the road. It chipped the windshield." John's eyes didn't leave the road, and she was suddenly glad he wasn't looking at her. His face was different, his demeanor rigid and hard. His eyes kept darting to the rearview, and she could see a light sheen on his forehead. "You okay?" he asked, his voice deep. "Bella," he growled when she didn't answer. "Are you injured?"

"No," she said, aghast as she took in the broken glass scattered over her baggage. "Your car, though. I think you need to pull over."

"I don't give a shit about the car," he said after a long pause. "As long as you're okay."

He drove a while up the freeway, the silence thick between them. The wind whipped through the broken glass. Every time she looked his way, he'd throw her an easy smile, but the atmosphere was different. It kept her silent.

They pulled off the highway and headed to a nondescript parking garage.

"Stay in the car," John breathed, pulling up into a space away from the other cars. "I just need to make a call. About the window."

He walked too far away for her to hear what he was talking about, so she sat and stared out the window.

It was too weird, the whole thing. She'd never seen a window get blown apart like that, and why didn't he stop? If that had happened to her, she would have pulled over right away. He'd driven like a mad man, and the whole thing felt off.

She looked around. They'd driven a good hour away, and she had no idea where they even were. It suddenly occurred to her that she was with a new man, who'd just driven her off to places unknown. No one knew where she was. Should she drop a pin to her agent, maybe? Call the kids?

"Hey." He pulled open her door and came to kneel before her. "I'm sorry about that. I…"

"Yeah, that was weird. I think maybe I should go home."

"No," he said a little too quickly. She jerked at his sharp tone. "No. Sorry." He puffed out a breath, running his hands through his short, cropped hair. "Listen, I didn't mean to scare you." He bit at his bottom lip, and she realized he was shaking.

"John, are you—"

"I'm fine. I just…listen." He reached for her hand, stopping just short of making contact with her skin and looking at her through half-hooded lids for permission. She bridged the gap, and he wrapped his fingers around hers. "I told you I was a consultant, which is true, but I didn't tell you where I consulted. I've been in some…tricky situations over the years, in some pretty dicey places. War zones," he added with a squeeze of his hand. "I kind of went into work mode when the bu—when the rock hit the car." He looked at her, his smile rueful. "Sometimes, we were in some pretty dodgy situations, and I guess I got used to being alert to anything unexpected. If you want me to take you home, I will, but the alarm company will have started by now. I would still like to spend the weekend with you. It will be better, I promise."

"You scared me a little," she admitted. "It was just a rock." He didn't acknowledge her. "But I get it, how the breaking glass could have triggered you. I wish you'd told me sooner. I had no idea you'd gone through things like that."

"I was just protecting you. I wish I could explain better, but…" His gaze turned dark again, pinning her to her seat. "Some things I don't want to talk about–can't. But I am a good guy. I will always look after you, Bella. You have to believe that. Everything I do, no matter how strange, it's all for you." He slowly brought her hand to his lips, looking as if he was expecting her to run from the car park screaming. "I will do what you want. I have another car coming, but I will drive you straight home if that's what you want."

CHAPTER
FIFTEEN
BELLA

The new car was there within the hour, with a silent, rather chiseled man behind the wheel.

As John transferred the bags to the new car, and the new guy looked at the damage like he was a crime scene investigator, Bella realized for the first time that her idea of John's job wasn't quite what she thought. She'd believed he sat behind a computer all day, selling and designing fancy house alarms and security systems for large corporations.

The beefcake who nodded at John before driving away in the damaged set of wheels looked more like John Cena than a Bill Gates type. He spoke in grunts only, and John's low tones in response made his big, thick head nod.

More than once, he looked Bella's way. If she didn't know any better, she would have thought they were discussing her. Maybe John told him he'd had a freak-out on the motorway. Perhaps, they used to work together.

The thing was, even while freaking out, John had been assertive. Sure of himself. It really was like some kind of battle training had kicked in. Knowing that, and given his explanation, it made sense. If she'd known he was some kind of war veteran from the beginning, she wouldn't have held it against him. His organized demeanor, the way he always seemed to be aware of his surroundings. Private security firms worked in war zones all the time. She'd done enough research on the subject for one of her novels to understand that.

By the time he loaded up their stuff and came to sit next to her in the driver's seat, she'd already decided what she was going to do.

He didn't meet her eyes as he started the engine. "So, where am I driving you?"

CHAPTER
SIXTEEN
JOHN

It turned out, his idea for a day out was well received. He had been planning to come here, anyway, but now it was more important than ever to be out in public. To keep her away from the house as long as possible until one of his buddies had checked it.

He hadn't gone through Hannah this time, because he knew without a doubt that the man who had taken a pot shot at them was none other than the sadistic piece of shit, Cyrus Jennings. Which meant that either Jasper had sent him, or Jennings was moonlighting. The chances of Gerald Carmichael tracking down details for two hitmen was too unlikely to be credible. The fact he had found the agency in the first place was a testament to the kind of people he did business with, but few people had a hired killer on speed dial.

He'd spotted Cyrus on the camera as they were leaving her house, and his blood had run cold. When he saw the shot hit the back windscreen, knowing it was seconds from taking out Bella, he saw red. He'd freaked her out, but the alternative was far worse.

As they stood amongst the furnishings in the department

store, he had to focus on looking relaxed. Roman was on it. He trusted his old buddy from overseas. They'd run missions together in the past for a few different organizations. He worked like John did, clean and clear, with the same set of morals. The opposite of Jennings.

"You really want me to pick stuff out for your place?" Bella ran her fingers along a sideboard. "This is what you want to do?"

They'd driven back toward home, but not to Andersen Falls. When she'd told him she wanted to continue their weekend, his whole body had sagged in his seat. And when she'd told him she understood what had happened and would be there for him if he needed to talk, he'd taken her hand, only letting it go long enough to walk around the front of the car. He felt like locking her away from the world, but he resisted blowing his cover. He needed her close, and if he told her the truth, she would run from him and right into danger.

"Definitely." He papered an easy smile over the cracks of his worried features. "You have good taste, and my interior design skills aren't exactly evolved. This isn't bad, though, right?" He pointed to an ornament that looked like a shell coated in silver. It was sticking out of a wooden block suspended on a wire mount. He knew it looked hideous. "Beachy."

He kept his face straight for all of two seconds before laughing at Bella's look of pure horror.

"There's no hope for you."

"I told you," he laughed. "I need you, Bella."

"Come on," she giggled, taking him by the arm. "Let's start with some bedding that doesn't look like it came from a hotel."

———

BELLA

By the time they got back to John's place, Bella was exhausted.

"I don't think we left anything in the shops for anyone else." She rubbed at her sore shoulders, sinking into his hard couch. "I'm glad they're delivering everything. I couldn't have lugged it all in here."

"I'll deal with all that. Thanks for helping me." He sat down next to her, shucking off his shoes and rubbing at a heel. "This place is going to look great. You hungry?"

"Starving," she admitted. They'd grabbed a quick bite to eat in between stores, but that was hours ago. "Do you fancy booking somewhere?"

John frowned. "Well, not to be presumptuous, but you did bring your overnight bag. I figured we could order in tonight, stay here, and have a night in?"

"Sounds good to me. To be honest, the thought of getting dressed up to go out is pretty unappealing. I feel like we just ran a marathon."

The look of relief on his face told her she'd made the right decision.

"Me, too. Do you want to pick a movie? I'll get the menus." Passing her the remote, he went into the kitchen. "Wine? It's after six, not too scandalous."

"Sounds good. I'm going to Facetime the kids first."

She rang Evan's phone, and three little faces filled her screen.

"Hi, Mom." Evan frowned when he saw her. "Where are you?"

"Err…" John walked in with two glasses and a bottle, and

she pulled away from the screen. "Sorry," she mouthed before turning back to her progeny. "I went to a friend's house. One of the school moms, a PTA thing. Are you all having fun?"

"Brittany made us mac and cheese," Poppy chipped in, sticking her face in the middle of the screen. "It's not as good as yours, but we had ice cream after."

"Sounds nice. Is your dad there?"

Evan pulled the phone away, much to Poppy's annoyance. "No. He left pretty much after we got to grandma's house." His face was stony. "I don't even know why he bothers asking us to come."

"Poppy! Daisy! Do you want to do manicures?" Brittany's voice filtered through, and Poppy disappeared, chatting away in the background. Daisy rolled her eyes at the screen. "Better go, Brittany wants us. Bye, Mom. Love you."

"Bye, sweetie. Be nice to Brittany, okay?"

Evan grunted.

"It's not her fault, Evan. Be nice. Please."

"Fine," he grumbled. "See you tomorrow."

"Bye, honey." But he was already gone. She took the glass of cold white wine John held out with a grateful smile. "Thanks. Sorry I didn't tell them I was here. I don't know if the kids had mentioned you, and I didn't fancy dealing with Gerry this weekend."

"I get it. It's not his business, but I guess he has a say in who's around his kids."

"Does he?" She took a long sip of her wine, tossing her phone onto the cushion beside her. "I never got a say in Brittany making my kids food, looking after them while he picks them up and leaves them on their own with her." She half drained the glass, needing the buzz to quell her anger. "I like her, truth be known. He told her he was going through a divorce, that we lived together but weren't a couple. Made himself sound real good, being a selfless father trying to be there for his children. I confronted her when it came out."

"You did?"

Bella nodded. "Oh, I drove to the car showroom with all guns blazing. Walked in there all fired up, ready for blood. She took one look at me and burst into tears." She cringed at the memory. "Apologized to me. I couldn't be mad at her, after that. She still stayed with him, but she's not all bad. She's ambitious, and I do believe that she cares for him. Or his money, at least. But she's nice to the kids. Makes an effort. She even took Poppy shopping for clothes once, and she didn't try to change her. Evan and Daisy give her a pretty hard time, but they go there for Poppy's sake, really. She's too young to realize her dad's not the superhero every little girl thinks their dad is. I don't want to ruin that for her."

Taking the glass out of her hand, John clasped it between his. "That's because you're a good person."

"Am I? I feel like an idiot sometimes."

"I think you're pretty amazing." He brought his hands up to cup her face. "I get this urge to look after you whenever we're together. To make you happy." His thumb ran along her cheekbone. "I really like you, Bella."

"I like you, too."

He moved closer, pulling her to him. She went willingly, feeling the air change between them. When his lips touched hers, they ignited. He started off slow, little kisses on her lips and her cheeks, along her jawline. She felt the nip of teeth along her neck and moaned at the contact.

"If you want me to stop…" He mumbled against her skin.

"I don't," she sighed, taking his face in her hands and pulling his lips back to hers. He deepened the kiss with a growl, his tongue slipping past her lips, lighting the touch paper between them once more.

Pulling her onto his lap, she straddled him greedily, feeling the hard length of him against her clothing. Wanting more, she gasped, pulling at his shirt buttons. She got halfway down and moaned at the belt stopping her descent. Wrenching his lips from hers as her fingers wrapped around his belt, he stilled her hands.

"We should stop. I don't want to take advantage of you."

"You're not," she panted. "I want this, John. I want you." His eyes searched hers, looking almost black with lust.

"You don't know…there are things about me you might not like."

She searched his eyes, waiting for her brain to kick in and warn her. Urge her to get up, leave. It was silent. Satiated in his arms. "Do you have another girlfriend, or a secret family somewhere?"

A burst of laughter shot through him, the tension dulling across his features. "No. It's just me, Bella. There was no one before you."

"Then, I trust you. I know you've done things in your past. I can't imagine what you've seen. Endured. I have led an isolated life. Too much, really. My adventures are in the pages I write, but I know you're a good man, John. I feel it." She placed her hand over her heart. "In here."

When she whispered, "Take me to bed," his lips found hers once more. He hungrily sucked at her bottom lip as she rocked her hips against him, desperate to feel more of him. Snapping the last threads of his hesitation as desire took over, he wrapped his arms around her and lifted her off the sofa and into his arms. He kept his lips sealed to hers as he strode across the room, headed to the bedroom.

Lowering her onto the bed, he took a step back. Through the light from the partly open blinds, she watched as he pulled the shirt from the confines of his pants, showing off his broad, muscular chest. Scars–some looking like slashes, others circular–were dotted against his skin. He saw her staring.

"From the job," he muttered. "I don't like looking at them." He went to pick his shirt back up, but she rose to her feet, stopping him.

Leaning down, she kissed a long, puckered area of skin on his left pec. "Don't," she urged him. "It's part of you. I have things, too." She pulled the shirt from his hand, tossing it to the floor. Standing before him, she didn't feel the embarrassment she thought might come to the forefront.

She felt seen.

She undressed slowly, revelling in the intake of breath from John as she took off her bra. Standing there, only clad in panties, she took his hand and traced his fingers over the faded tiger stripes on her stomach. "From the kids," she murmured. "No one is perfect, John."

"You are," he huffed, dropping to his knees to kiss the skin he'd just traced. "You're perfect to me."

The rest of their clothing came off slowly, each teasing the other in the dark as they caressed the broken, damaged parts, and somehow healed them with each touch. Breathing ragged, they took their time, as if the world had been paused. In this place, apart from the rest of civilization, it had.

His cock sprang free when she released it from his boxers, a drop of pre-cum leaking from the tip. She rubbed it with her thumb, drawing a hiss from him as her hand stroked up and down.

"You drive me crazy." He reached for her, lifting her onto the bed and caging her in with his arms. "Sometimes, I have to remind myself you're really here." His eyes pinned her to the spot, passion radiating from them. "I know we haven't known each other long, but I will always be here. I will always protect you. I promise that with everything I have."

He drew her closer, skin on skin. Held her tight, like she was something so precious she might break in his grasp. He was different tonight. Had been the whole day, if she was honest. The accident on the road had rattled him far more than he let on. Seeing him like that, knowing more about him, she understood him better. She wanted to know him more, but realized that he might never show her those deepest, darkest parts of him. And that was okay, because she had already fallen for the ones he had offered to her. She saw the truth in the way he looked at her, shielded her.

"I believe you," she told him, in between kisses. He ran his hands over her body, cupping her and running his thumbs against her nipples until she begged him for more. When his fingers slid inside her, she was desperate. Mewling, moaning as he curled them up against her wall, finding the perfect spot. She felt the pleasure build as he finally made contact with her bud, stroking it in small circles and building the tension until it threatened to consume her. She bucked her hips against his hand, reaching for his hard length. She stroked him as he moaned and huffed out frantic breaths.

"Jesus," he groaned. "Keep touching me like that and I won't last." He grabbed her hand, pinning it above her head. Entwining his fingers in hers as he coaxed out her release, his hand was wet from her arousal. "I need you to come for me first. Come all over my hand. I want to hear you screaming my name as you come for me."

That was all it took. The tension grew white hot in her belly, and his name burst from her lips as her orgasm shattered through her. John's smile was jubilant as he watched her lose control underneath him. "You're so fucking beautiful." His fingers slowed, and she mourned the absence of his touch as he finally pulled away. "Hearing my name on your lips is the sexiest sound in the world." He kissed her again, hard, his tongue meeting hers. "I'll never have enough of this."

Coming down from the clouds, she reached for his length again. As she touched him, she revelled in the groan she elicited from him. "I want more, too," she confessed. "I'm still on birth control. And I got tested."

She didn't say why she'd tested. She didn't need to.

"Are you sure?" he checked. "I'd like nothing more than to feel you with nothing." His face was almost rueful. "But I– I didn't plan for this. I don't have protection."

She smiled against his lips, bringing the head of his cock to her wet folds. "You're all the protection I need."

He made a noise that came from the very depths of him, and kissing her hard, he pushed in. Slowly, inch by inch, she felt him shudder as he sheathed himself fully inside her. "God, baby. You're so wet. You feel so good, taking me like this. Like you're made for me, baby."

He pulled out slowly, in and out, driving her half mad. He whispered how stunning and sexy she was in her ear as his teeth skimmed her neck, nipping, sucking, and laving where his teeth had been with his tongue. She pulled him closer, needed him nearer, deeper. Her hands ran down his corded, scarred back and cupped his buttocks as she rose up to meet him with her hips.

"Look at me, baby," he urged when her eyelids closed. "Keep your eyes on mine while I make you come again. One more." His hand came down between them as he threw her leg over his shoulder, making her gasp. He was in so deep, hitting the magic button inside her while his callused fingers stroked her clit. He felt like he was everywhere, her hand still joined with his as he kissed her. He only pulled back to meet her gaze as his thrusts grew more erratic.

"Come with me," she begged him, high on the thrill of seeing this man who was so strong and sure look so vulnerable and undone as he pounded into her. He moaned again, gripping her hand tighter as he gazed down into those dark eyes, half lidded and hazy.

"Oh Jesus, Bella. You feel so good. Gripping me so tight." He dipped his neck, sucking near her collarbone as he panted hard against her skin. "I wish you were mine."

Those were the words she thought she heard him whisper, but her orgasm hit before she could get a handle on them. She answered him, anyway. Her mind had already been screaming it. As she fell apart around him, she told him over and over as her whole body tingled, "I'm yours, John. I'm yours."

The second she uttered it, he thrust harder, his hand moving to her hip as he roared with his own release. She felt him come, a shuddering of his hips as he released her hand and lifted her back off the mattress to cage his arms around her. They lay there, wrapped in each other. Panting. Sticky. Spent.

Once their breathing returned to some semblance of normal, he kissed her tenderly, slowly, as if he was trying to bring them both back down to the ground. Eventually, he pulled back, lifting her off the bed as if she weighed nothing.

"What are you doing?" she laughed as he pulled back the covers.

"I'm going to snuggle with my girlfriend until I get my strength back, and then we're going to do that again."

She smirked at him as he moved them both back onto the mattress, tucking her in so he was flush against her back. Dropping a kiss on her shoulder, he wrapped her in his arms. Warm and cozy, she felt her eyelids droop as she settled in against him. "Girlfriend, eh?"

"After what we just did, you're damn right you're my

girlfriend." He paused, and she felt him tense. It was barely there, but something about this man made her hyper aware of everything he did. "You said you were mine." The statement was uncharacteristically cautious, the unsure tone coating his soft words as they lay together in the dark. "Did you mean that?"

"Yes," she smiled, before sleep pulled her under. "I'm yours, John, and you're mine."

CHAPTER
SEVENTEEN
JOHN

This is more than a job. It's always been more.

In all the years, in all the contracts he'd executed, he'd never been conflicted. Not once. He'd done his due diligence, and he was sure when he pulled the trigger that he was doing the right thing. Never had he lost sleep after completing a task. Never once, in all the corners of the world, had he laid in bed and struggled to sleep.

Even with Bella in his bed, her soft snores against his neck hadn't induced slumber. Being with her all night, reaching for each other in the darkness, he'd never felt more loved. Seen. They'd exhausted each other, and he'd made her come. So many times, with his mouth and his body. He couldn't get enough of her, the way she looked at him as he drove into her.

You're mine, John. Three words that had brought him so much joy. He'd felt like punching the air when she'd said it. It wasn't just a reaction to the claim on her he'd blurted out. She felt it, just as much as he did. He knew it. Could tell. He'd never had that, had never made love to a woman and felt the connection between them grow and spill over. It was like the moon and stars had aligned. The way she moaned his name when he was between her thighs, driving her again and again to tumble over the edge…

Jesus, he was Mr Sappy. He couldn't get enough of her, in bed and out. They'd made love to each other in the early morning, showered together. They hadn't even lasted long enough under the steam without succumbing to the pure heat between them. She'd screamed his name under the hot spray of water as he'd pounded into her against the tile. She loved his body and didn't baulk at his scars. She'd kissed every inch of him. Accepted him.

I would die for her. Without a doubt in my mind, I would take each and every bullet that came her way. As long as she was okay, he'd die a happy man. Having known her touch and felt her affection, it would be enough to sustain him for eternity. *She's mine, and I protect what's mine.*

They'd driven back to her place Sunday afternoon, and he'd waited in the kitchen as Gerry dropped the kids off. He'd parked down the street, both of them knowing without saying a word to the other that they wanted this bubble to last as long as possible. John knew Gerry hadn't seen the replacement car, but the fact he didn't have to explain his new ride still eased the gut wrenching guilt he felt about hiding things from her.

Gerry was rattled, John could hear it in his voice. His tone was clipped, snappy when he spoke to Bella, but she didn't rise to it, ever the watchful, caring mother. John would have given anything to see his face. He could tell by the surprise in Gerry's voice that he hadn't expected her to open the door. The bastard had brought his kids back, all the while hoping their mother was gone. Not even thinking about what it would do to their children, only caring about his own ends. John had gripped the kitchen counter to stop himself from running to the front door and choking him out right there on the doorstep. So, he enjoyed the audio of the man's discomfort and irritation instead, knowing the days of Gerry thinking he was going to get his way were numbered.

Jennings hadn't been to the house. He wasn't that stupid. While Bella slept, John had checked the cameras and touched base with his buddy. Roman had tagged his vehicle, tracked him, and reported back. He knew Jennings had worked out by now that she wasn't alone this weekend.

What he didn't know was that John was coming for him.

He'd left after Sunday dinner, and Roman stood watch over the house to keep Bella and the kids safe. John had squashed down the guilt he felt as she'd pulled him into the hallway alcove to kiss him goodbye. He was loathed to leave her, for more reasons than he could ever tell her. But she had the kids to see to, and he'd told her the truth. That he had some work to do.

This weekend had been too close for comfort. He'd kept her safe, but it wasn't easy. Having to conceal the fact she'd dodged a bullet? He couldn't do that forever. Couldn't be with her 24/7. Not yet. Their relationship was new, and he wasn't about to lose her by turning into what looked like a possessive stalker.

And it wasn't just about her. There were the kids to think about. They could have been in the car. Jennings wouldn't have cared. He'd shoot his own grandmother in the face for a few thousand dollars and not blink an eye. John needed to protect the three tiny humans he was getting to know and growing to really like.

They were all getting under his skin, and it was keeping him up. He couldn't sleep, because their father was trying to take out their mother to save his fucking reputation and the integrity of his bank balance. He'd taken the job to save his favorite writer, to stop someone else from taking the job. Now, they were family to him. The second he'd seen Bella, he'd been in this. Hadn't been able to stay professional, and hadn't wanted to.

But Gerry wasn't giving up. The arrogant SOB had hired someone else, even after their little chat in the gym, and they wouldn't be the last. He could tell Bella the truth, and she could go to the police, but then what? They'd never prove it. John would have to disappear. It's what he should do, to protect them, but he already knew he wouldn't. He couldn't do it. He was too invested, and there wasn't a man on the planet who could protect them better than he could.

Jennings had to go, and then he'd deal with Gerry.

The hotel was shitty, nothing like the places John had holed up in whilst on jobs. He never booked the Hilton, but he at least avoided roach motels like the dive he was currently staring at through the windshield of his new rental car. The scrap of crap inside owed him for that, too.

Instead of being with Bella, he was sitting in the dark, waiting to strike once more. This time was different, though. It was against one of his own, no less. Even if he hadn't been leaving the day job, tonight's actions would certainly blacklist him from the business. *Persona non grata.* After tonight, there would be no more employee discount club, that was for certain. An unsanctioned execution of a colleague was bad etiquette in their line of work, even when it was a waste of skin like Cyrus.

Tucking his Glock out of sight, he stuck to the shadows, and avoided the lighting from the street. The cameras were all broken, the blinking lights just for show. His instincts tuned in to the quiet of the parking lot and the hum of the air conditioning units as he passed the window of each motel room. There was the blare of various television sets, the occasional shout from the occupants inside. A couple in Room 38 were going at it like a couple of wildcats. They wouldn't hear a bomb going off right now if it exploded next to them.

Pausing after the door of Room 42, he pushed himself against the wall, adjusting the brim of his baseball cap lower on his face. He could hear the low hum of the radio from Room 43. Jazz.

I hate jazz, he winced to himself.

It was all just white noise to him, anyway. Perhaps, that was the point. He listened in and was rewarded with Jennings's dulcet tones.

"I couldn't get close. I'm telling you, she has protection."

He was talking to someone. Jasper or Gerry? John's hand tightened on the barrel of his gun.

"Yeah, well, the plates were fake. Some old lady in Encino. From the way they hauled ass, it wasn't Miss Daisy driving. I lost them after two blocks, and there was no trace of the car after that. The cameras didn't ping the plates, so I'm guessing they bailed. I thought you said this was some housewife?"

Whatever the caller said back, it made Jennings explode.

"Jasper, I need the truth. I don't like being surprised on the job, and this place is some cookie cutter town. I want out. The money's not enough as it is." Another pause. "Yes, I want more money!" John could hear him pacing around the room, listening to whatever Jasper said. "You told me this was a quick in and out," he grumbled. "I could have taken that Korea job, and I'd be eating sushi right now with a mill in the bank instead of cheap ass takeout in some slum." Silence. "Yeah? Well, you have me till tomorrow. Wire me the extra tonight or the deal's off." John heard the scrape of something across a tabletop. "Screw Jasper. Asshole."

John slid his skeleton key card into the slot and pushed

the door open wide. "You're both assholes," he said coldly. Kicking the door shut behind him, he pointed the gun at Jennings' head. "Jasper gave you my contract?"

Jennings stood there in a pair of jeans. The bottle of Jack he'd been holding thudded to the floor as he lunged for his gun on the side table. John was faster, cracking him across the head with the butt of his own gun before he managed to take two steps.

"Hey!" Jennings grunted as he hit the floor. John took aim at a kneecap and fired, the silencer muffling the shot. "Jesus!" Jennings screamed, dragging himself to the foot of the bed, a trail of blood flowing from his obliterated joint.

John punched him across the face. "Scream again, and the next one will be in your head. Make any noise, and your other kneecap is a goner." Keeping the gun trained on him, John sauntered across to the chair in the corner, picking up the whiskey bottle on his way and pouring its contents on the bullet wound. Jennings turned purple, clamping a pillow over his mouth to quell his cries of agony.

John took a swig, nodding as if he was having a drink with a buddy. "Not bad." He waved the square bottle at the man on the floor. "I prefer brandy, but a nice Jack now and then really takes the edge off." He trained the gun at Jennings' intact knee. "Why did Jasper hire you, Cyrus? This job is off limits."

Jennings pushed his sweat-soaked hair off his face, leaving a blood smear across his blotchy forehead. "I don't know!"

"Liar, liar, pants on fire," John sang, cocking the trigger.

"I'm not, I'm not!" he squeaked. John raised a gloved finger to his lips, shushing him. "I'm not lying. I don't know why. He just said someone pulled out of the job, so I had to do it. He offered me a good deal."

John's tongue stroked the inside of his cheek as he kept his fury in check. He'd already figured Jasper was behind it. He'd dismissed it at first, but it made sense. Jasper had realized Bella meant something to John, and he thought by taking her out, John would change his mind about his retirement. Fueled by anger, he'd have come back to the fold and done Jasper's dirty work forevermore. He'd give him this—Jasper was nothing if not pragmatic about his bottom line. Bumping off a woman to keep his best earner close; that was low, even for him. It was a shame he was going to have to retire himself now. Jasper had pulled his last dirty trick.

"How much?"

Jennings, teeth clenched and wild eyed, grunted with pain as he answered. "Hundred," he gritted out. "I didn't know you were on it." His brows dipped as the details came back to him. "Why didn't you take the target out? You in protection now or something?"

"Yeah," John smiled as he raised the gun and shot Jennings between the eyes. "And I protect what's mine."

———

Clean-up was the worst. He should have sent his old cleaning crew a Christmas bonus or something. He did the hits, but cleaning up the scenes? It was rare, and only when necessary. Like today.

The smell of bleach still clung to him, a cloying burn in his nostrils as he closed the furnace door. Andersen Falls Crematorium was very lax in their security. Jennings would be laid to rest, but in someone else's urn.

When he got back to the car, John waited until he was out of range of the block's security cameras and rebooted the CCTV. He could see the plume of white smoke in his rear view as he dialed Roman's number. "Bye bye, Jennings. Rest in peace."

When the call connected, John didn't wait for a greeting. "It was him."

"Jesus," Roman sighed. "So much for an easy retirement. Handled your end?"

"Yep. Up in smoke."

Roman chuckled. "Well, you know what they say."

"There's no smoke without fire," John replied, giving him the signal. A second later, a huge boom sounded in his ear as Roman triggered the bomb that would take out Jasper. "I owe you one, brother."

"Any time."

Heading for home, John drew a full breath for the first time that weekend. Two problems solved, one to go. Picking up the burner phone from the passenger seat, he dialed another number.

"Hello?" Gerry's weedy voice made him want to punch the steering wheel.

"I told you not to fuck with me, Gerald."

The line went silent.

"I–I didn't. Someone contacted me."

"I know, and they're dead. Mess with Bella again, and you'll join them."

Breaking the phone in half, he threw it out of the window. Maybe tonight, he might just get some rest. His phone beeped, and his heart leaped out of his chest as he read the message.

A shower and a fresh change of clothes later, he slunk silently through the night, staying in the shadows. As he reached the front door, it opened.

"Hey, baby." He smiled, pulling Bella in for the kiss he'd thought about all day. "Secret sleepover, huh? My favorite."

"Shush." She laughed, pulling him inside and locking the door behind them. "I couldn't sleep. Did you get your work done?"

"Mission accomplished." He bent at the waist, throwing her over his shoulder and heading to the stairs. She squealed, and he slapped her on her sleep shirt clad behind to silence her. "Now, little Miss Insomnia, let's see if your boyfriend can rock you to sleep."

CHAPTER
EIGHTEEN
BELLA

She should have known it was too good to be true. The children hadn't told Gerry about John, because he had been quiet for the last few weeks. They hadn't been back to see him since that weekend, and they were happier for it. Maybe he really was going to leave them alone now. If she could just get him to sign the papers, it would all be over.

John was around all the time now. They went out for dinner, and Erin watched the kids if they wanted to be alone. He slept over most nights, leaving before the kids woke up, but she knew the time would come soon that he'd be there with them. Having breakfast. Being a normal couple.

The kids loved him. He came to all of Evan's games, had helped Daisy with her coding homework more than once, and Poppy was his shadow. Life was good, great even.

She was falling in love with John, and having the best sex of her life. She still blushed when she looked at the kitchen island, remembering when she'd come back from the school run and he'd been waiting to bend her over the counter. "I missed you, baby," he'd whispered in her ear as he then proceeded to show her just how much.

She and the kids had spent time at his place, helping him to put his furniture in place and eating pizza on his couch while watching Disney movies, at Poppy's insistence. Bella had caught him singing one of the Moana songs in the car just the day before. When she'd teased him about it, he'd raised a Dwayne Johnson brow and sung even louder. Things had been so perfect, she'd stopped waiting for the other shoe to drop.

And then, the email dropped.

So, this sunny Monday morning, she dropped the kids off at school and found herself walking into the room the PTA used. As soon as she strode through the door, she heard that damn proverbial shoe hit the floor.

It looked normal, at first. She'd felt confident, walking in there. Freshly sexed up by John, who'd dropped her off, and wearing a new dress that showed off her curves, she was ready to face the coven and maybe even make some amends. Until she came face to face with Chrissie, and then her good mood evaporated like water in a cauldron.

"Bella," she beamed, looking every inch a Stepford Wife, the Glenn Close version. "So glad you could make it."

The air was so thick Bella wondered who'd died. Or who had made a social faux pas deemed unacceptable by the cliquey bitches surrounding the refreshments table like the pack of jackals they were.

"What's wrong?"

That was the worst thing she could have said. She should have chosen something banal, like, "Did you see the sale on at Sephora, ladies? What about those Costco deals, huh? Crazy!"

Half the clan immediately found the tips of their heels infinitely interesting. The core group, the mid-life crisis cohort, smelled blood in the water, homing in on her face with their immaculately made-up sneers. Chrissie, as per usual, took the lead.

"Oh, nothing really." She waved a hand in the direction of the group. "We just wanted to raise a concern." She licked her lips. "About Poppy."

Fire licked up her spine. *Here we go*, she thought, preparing to tell this bunch of ill-meaning crones to back the fuck up. "What about Poppy?" She folded her arms, taking a defensive stance and feeling her hackles rise. *Don't poke the mama bear, Chrissie.*

"Well, we did notice the poster on the noticeboard. Things seem to be getting out of hand, don't you think?"

There it was. Bella had seen it, too, before the weekend, before she'd ripped it down and thrown it into the nearest bin. It was a polite notice reminding students that the 'correct' attire should be worn by all students. Nothing controversial there, but the images were what had grabbed her attention. Stereotypical images of a boy in board shorts, blue T-shirt, and baseball cap, next to a demure and mindless-looking girl with a floral dress and Mary Jane shoes. Holding a flower. As if girls couldn't board or have anything other than a vapid look plastered across their baby doll faces.

She nodded, feeling the urge to knock the look of fake concern right off Chrissie's face. Preferably with a pool ball in a sock. That would sort out those perfect, slightly too shiny, slightly too big for her smart mouth veneers.

"I saw that, too." She cocked her head. "Same font as what the PTA usually prefers to use, I noticed. Comic Sans. You should look into that. People might get the wrong idea."

Chrissie's eye twitched, right on cue. "Exactly. The wrong idea. I just think–*we* just think…" She glared at the bunch of vaginas around her, and they all nodded on command.

"Poppy, bless her heart, might benefit from…you know…. dressing for her gender."

Bella sighed, holding back the maniacal laugh she felt coursing through her. She was going to write a thriller one day, she decided. And in it, she would murder the head of the PTA in the most delicious way possible. Then, she'd send Chrissie a damn fruit basket with a signed copy nestled against the wicker.

"Poppy is fine with how she dresses, and so am I."

A chorus of *aww* and *oh no, she's fine* rose up, but Chrissie cut them off with a raise of her hand. She took a step closer to Bella, standing her ground. Bella knew what was coming. The look on Chrissie's face screamed, "Bend to my will," while Bella made her face the perfect expression of, "Back the heck up."

"And, of course, Poppy should be able to express her unique personality, but we–" Another glare over her shoulder. "–just think that she's open to a lot of scrutiny, and we are obviously concerned. What with the poster and everything."

"I don't care about the poster, and unless the principal contacts me directly with his concerns, Poppy will be coming to school wearing what she wants. She's a kid. She doesn't want to be a boy, and she's not confused about her identity."

She clenched her teeth, recalling the conversation she'd had to have when the poster had been put on the noticeboard. She still cringed when remembering last night, when her daughter had paused her computer game to look at her blankly.

"Ugh, Mom, no. You are so cringe. I'm not a boy."

Bella had tripped over her words, eager to not alienate her daughter by saying the wrong thing. She'd been reading up online, wanting to be supportive and avoid scaring her child into clamming up about something that might be a life-changing revelation. "Well, if you were, that would be totally fine, too. We love you, no matter what you want or need to be."

Poppy had laughed. "I know that, Mom. God, you're so silly. I know about trans people. Isaac said his Auntie Jo turned into his Uncle Jo, and we talked about it in class. I don't want to be a boy. They suck!" She shoveled a gummy worm into her mouth, chewing thoughtfully. "Immy asked me if I was trans, too, but I told her: I'm a girl, I want to be a girl. I just don't want to have to wear girly stuff. Why should I?" She looked down at her current outfit, which consisted of a Ninja Turtles T-shirt and a pair of Gap boys jeans. Her hair was hidden away by a backward baseball cap. "Boys have way cooler stuff, and they get to game and skateboard."

Bella had sat down on the bed, dropping a kiss on top of her daughter's hatted head. "I know, love, but girls can do those things, too. I just wanted to…oh, I don't know. I wanted to check in. I know school can be tricky."

Poppy paused her game again. "School's cool. All my friends are okay with it." She'd tapped her chin with the controller. "And if they weren't, so what? I don't care."

Bella's chest felt warm. "How did I get such a fab kid, huh? I swear, I blinked and you've practically turned into a teenager. You're so grown up."

Poppy shrugged. "Yeah, well, I'm nearly six. That's major." Bella could see her own eyes staring back at her. "When I'm as old as you, I don't want to be boring. That would suck."

Bella had laughed, dropping a kiss on the tip of her youngest's nose, wondering when her kids stopped being babies, and how they were doing so much better at knowing who they were than she did at their age. "That would suck," she agreed. "As long as you're happy, Pops."

"She's happy with who she is," she told the PTA ladies, now, pulling herself out of the memory and hating the fact that she'd been forced to do it in the first place by women who were less mature than a child. "She dresses how she feels most comfortable."

"Yes," Chrissie countered. "But if you took her to the right clothing stores–"

"Then, she wouldn't buy anything. Poppy has dressed like this since she was old enough to tell me what she didn't like. She used to borrow Evan's clothes until I bought her own. And if you didn't make the poster, why are you so bothered by this? Huh?"

Twitch, twitch. Chrissie's eyelid was having its own little twerking party.

Pru side-stepped Chrissie, looking more than a little uncomfortable. "I can see we have hit a nerve, but as part of the PTA, we–"

"No." Bella pushed her palm out in front of her, feeling more than a little irked. "The PTA does not have the right to railroad a little girl. Have you not seen the news about the trans movement? Do you not realize how sensitive a subject it is? To call out a child for expressing herself? It's disgusting. I can tell you now, I will not have another conversation about this. Take those posters down, or I will be making a formal complaint against each and every one of you." She turned to Chrissie, who was staring at her, mouth open. "And as for you, carry on with this stupid petty backbiting, and I will make sure to contact your husband and his office and tell them just what his wife and her band of bitches are up to." She ran her hands down her dress, pulling herself together. "Now, if you'll excuse me, I have a lunch date to get to." *A naked one.* John was just the man to turn her day the right way around.

She was pushing through the doors when Chrissie called after her, "Yes, well, when I called your husband this morning to invite him to the meeting, he was very interested to hear about your new man, so maybe you should focus more on your kids and less on your love life!"

Bella turned to look back at her, fixing her with the deadliest stare she could muster. "Thanks for the advice, Chrissie, but the last person I would take parenting tips from is you. As for my boyfriend, the kids love him, and I think we all know that Gerry made his way around town before we split up. Who I date now is none of his, or your, business." She bit her lip, thinking of something Daisy had once told her. The old Bella would have slunk out of there and not said a word, but the new Bella Carmichael was ready with a bullet in the chamber. "And the next time you go and get the fat sucked out of your ass, telling everyone you're on a yoga retreat, tell them to fix your nose, too. The one you have must be worn out, getting stuck in everyone's business."

Chrissie's twitch spread to her whole face, and Bella stifled a laugh as she saw the other moms all turn to look at their leader, aghast. "See you around, ladies!" She saluted Chrissie. "Bye, Felicia!"

She didn't drop her smile as she left school. She beamed at her neighbor as he pulled up to the house, waving as she shut the front door behind her and sagged behind it. The second she saw John, it crumpled.

"What's wrong?" he asked, taking one look at her expression before folding her into his warm embrace. "Did they try to turn you into a pod person?"

"Worse," she replied, bursting into tears. "They're coming after Poppy. They made a stupid poster about dressing like a girl. I told them where to get off, but I lost my temper. Chrissie won't let it go until she gets her way." She groaned, taking another sip. "And Chrissie also took it upon herself to invite Poppy's dad to the meeting, and she told Gerald about you and me."

John didn't say anything for a moment, he just held her tighter. For a second, fear crept in. The irrational fear that this could push him away. Problems with the kids was one thing, but having an ex-husband in the picture that knew he existed? She couldn't help but worry that this new development could finally be the pin to burst their bubble. Sniffing, she pulled herself together and met his eye, ready for his reaction.

"I'm glad he knows. It's about time. It's a small town, so I'm surprised he didn't hear something already, to be honest. We can get out in front of it. Don't worry about it. I'm not. Gerry has nothing to do with us, and I won't let him hurt you anymore."

"You don't know what he can be like. With the divorce–"

"I know enough." He wrapped his arms around her like a security blanket. *Her* security blanket. "I'm not scared of Gerald and his tantrums." Leading her to the couch, he took her purse and poured her a glass of wine.

"It's barely noon," she chided, drinking half of it.

"I'll drive to pick the kids up," he smiled, placing a kiss on her temple. "Besides, I might just have an idea."

———

Carpool would never be the same. It would forever be changed after this uneventful Tuesday morning turned into something Andersen Falls would not forget in a hurry. Bella could see the cars, all stalled in one long, silent line. On a normal school day, the carpool attendants would be there in full force, hi-vis vests and radios bringing their implied superiority crashing to the forefront of their psyches. Their beady eyes would be glaring at the parents who dared to take a second longer than deemed necessary to drop off their progeny. Taking an extra second to kiss your offspring goodbye? Sacrilege. If you lingered more than once, a strongly worded email would be sent to you the same day, explaining the rules and regulations of car pool, which weren't that hard to follow in the first place. If cattle could follow it, so could humans raising humans, right?

Carpool had to be one of the easiest and most mind-numbingly boring parts of parenting. It was right up there with the horror of the PTA cult and The Wiggles. Carpool was control, conformity wrapped up in a smiling, secure package. Drop off and leave, drop off and leave. Kids on a conveyor belt of cars and SUVs. It demanded a uniformed drop-off and collection, and anything else was penalized swiftly and smugly. And if you messed with the cones? Well, you'd be cancelled by school culture, possibly shot at dawn. No one had ever seen that dad in the Dodge Charger who'd crumpled a couple of them last semester. He probably slept with the fishes now, tied to the bottom of the ocean by a concrete-filled orange cone.

But not today. Today, the carpool was as still as the freeway post zombie apocalypse. Even the stern attendants were frozen in time, holding radios limp by their sides as they watched John and Poppy striding toward the school. For her viewpoint in the car park, Bella watched through the windshield as Poppy skipped up the steps. Skipped. Bella didn't know the little girl even knew how before now, and she felt like dancing herself. She watched the man in her life walk her daughter into school without a care in the world, Poppy zinging with energy at his side, her little hand wrapped in his, and John's head dipping down every once in a while as if to check on her. Which Bella knew he was. Something about John was always watchful, protective. It made her heart soar. Along with her libido. Honestly, she'd never found him so attractive.

Her handsome boyfriend, looking gigantic at the side of her daughter as they held hands–him in his chosen outfit, Poppy in a dress of her own–was the one stopping all the traffic.

The sequins on his top sparkled in the morning sun, high-lighting his toned, tanned, and fuzz-free legs. He looked like he was having fun, shoulders straight back, gait relaxed. He rocked the heels he wore, a pair of black heels to match the flowing skirt he'd picked out at Walmart the night before.

Bella was so gone for this man. They all were. He was going to bat for Poppy so hard that he'd gone to school dressed as a woman just to prove a point to the PTA. When he'd issued the challenge to Poppy about wearing a dress, she'd thought he was joking.

Now, watching the pair of them disappear from view into the building, she realized that for once in her life, Bella was really living. Her children were thriving and happy, and she had a man like this to share her life with. A man who would shop for a sequin top and wear it into the den of wolves, just to show her daughter she didn't have to change herself if she didn't want to. It might be the last day Poppy wore a dress, and Bella was okay with that. Because she knew that what-ever happened, they would all deal with it. Together.

"You were amazing!" She laughed as he reappeared, taking yet another photo of him as he sank into the passenger seat.

"Poppy laughed the whole way there, and I'm pretty sure one of the teachers looked up my skirt," he huffed, making Bella guffaw. "It's not funny. I feel violated!"

"Welcome to being a woman," she giggled, grabbing him to kiss his face. "I think you look pretty sexy. The shaved legs were a nice touch."

John groaned, but his grin was infectious. "I saw Chrissie on the way out."

"Oh yeah? What did she say?"

"Nothing," he smirked back. "She was too busy staring." He chuckled. "But I definitely saw her eye twitch when I asked her for the name of her yoga retreat."

Bella exploded, and it took them a good ten minutes to stop laughing enough to drive back home.

Gerald was waiting when they pulled up to the house. Bella's jubilant mood was devoured by the stomach acid that rose from the pit of her stomach. He'd pulled his car into the driveway like he still lived there, and the arrogant move made her foot clench on the brake as she pulled in next to him. He was leaning against the front door, trying to peer through the glass, and when he turned to face them, his face fell. Bella could see the utter shock on his face. She steeled herself for a showdown.

"I'd better go talk to him." She went to get out of the car, but John's hand gently touched her arm.

"No. We'll go together. Wait here."

Bella clenched her keys tight in her fist as John stepped out, his eyes never leaving Gerry's as he came to her door and reached for her hand. Of all the times her ex could have met her boyfriend, she never imagined it would be when he was wearing a skirt. Gerry's face was ashen, but when he finally slid his eyes from John's to hers, she stood tall. John tucked her into his side, his stance protective.

"Gerald, this is John, my new boyfriend." There was no point in small talk. She knew why he was here. Gerald was frozen on the spot, looking John up and down as if he didn't trust his own eyes. "He, er–there is a reason he's dressed like this. Poppy was having some trouble at school."

Gerry blinked. "Christine called me." His gaze slid back to John's. He was eyeing him like a hiker would a bear in their path. "How long has this been going on?"

"A while now," John cut in, holding out his hand. "John Smith. Bella's partner."

Partner. Not boyfriend. Bella had to hide the shiver of happiness that bubbled up at hearing those words.

Gerry nodded dumbly, staring at his outstretched hand.

"To what do we owe the pleasure?" John continued. "Come to sign the divorce papers?"

Gerry's eyes darkened, and Bella looked from man to man. Something was off. John was acting strange. She could feel the tension rolling off him.

"No," Gerry stammered. "I c-came to talk to my wife. Alone."

John's hand lowered, and he took a step forward. "She's not your wife anymore, Gerry. I think you should leave."

Gerry took a step back, but he puffed up his chest like a wet bird. "I don't want any trouble."

"There's no trouble." Bella tried to get between them, but John pulled her back to his side, shielding her. "John! What's gotten into you? Gerry, I'm sorry, but you shouldn't be here. My lawyer said–"

Gerry, looking like he was going to throw up, started to back up to his car. "I don't care about the lawyers." He raised a shaky finger at John. "I don't want him near my kids, Bella."

John snarled, making Bella jump. When she looked at him, standing there dressed like that, he still looked foreboding. Feral.

"I'm not signing anything, you hear me, John? You don't scare me!" Gerry fumbled for his keys, clambering into his car as John advanced on him. The tires squealed as he backed out of the drive, slamming into a trash can as he peeled off down the street.

When the roar of his engine receded, John turned to face her.

"What the hell was that?" Bella huffed, pulling out her house key.

He shook his head, looking at the ground.

"Why did you have to say that? You know he can cause real trouble for me and the kids. I'm still tied to him!"

"I'm sorry, I didn't…" He stopped, heaving a sigh. "I was protecting you."

"Protecting me? You made things worse!" Gripping her house key, she brushed away a tear.

There it was. The other shoe.

"I want to be on my own, John."

"Bella, no–"

"Yes!" She bellowed. "I can't do this right now! He's probably on the phone to my solicitor now, telling them you've threatened him!"

"I'll make it right."

She couldn't look at him. She was too upset. Gerry had tried to control and ruin her life again, but it wasn't just hers. The kids would be caught in the crossfire. She was stupid for not telling him about John in the first place. She always had to do the right thing, yet Gerry did what he liked and held all the cards.

It was over. The bubble had finally burst.

"I don't think we can, now, John. He won't let this drop. I just…I need some time. Please, just go."

She didn't wait for an answer. She left him standing there on the driveway, locking the door behind her. The quiet of the house enveloped her.

"Alone again," she sighed. "I should have known."

CHAPTER
NINETEEN
JOHN

John's palms were slick with sweat. He could feel it through his gloves as he held his gun. He'd done this so many times, in many different places. Been in some sticky situations, where his life and the lives of countless others hung in the balance. The piece of shit in his other hand, however, posed the biggest threat.

"Please, take my wallet. My watch, it's a Rolex!"

John clocked him on the side of the head, shutting him up with a weak whimper. "It's a Folex, dipshit. Talk again and I'll shoot you in the jaw." He kept his voice low, Batman style. He didn't want to spoil the surprise just yet. He needed this guy to know, without a shadow of a doubt, that he was screwed, and that he was never to mess with anyone or anything John cared about ever again. "Get in. Now."

His eyes were wild as he looked around the dark, deserted lot. There was no one about, but John saw his eyes flick up frantically to the CCTV mounted nearby.

John chuckled, making the man quivering in his grasp turn to stare at him. Not that he could see anything but a pair of black eyes beneath the thick woollen balaclava. "In the van." He nodded his head toward the open side of the nondescript white vehicle, and he knew from the way his captive tensed that he'd clocked the bucket inside the door, along with the thick coil of rope. "I wouldn't count on the cameras, either. I pulled the feed for the whole block."

Gerald's eyes went wide, the whites visible even against the dark. John had also cut the lights to the lot, but they would be back up along with the video feeds after they were long gone. No trace of what had gone down would be left. Clean in and out. Another day at the office.

Gerald was still snivelling, wasting time. Losing patience, John gave him a hard shove. With his hands bound, he barely managed to break his fall. The bucket skittered across the floor of the van as John jumped in, sliding the door closed.

"Careful with your toilet there. You break that and you'll have nothing to crap in." Gerald looked at the rolling bucket with horror as it came to a slow stop on its side. "Legs out in front of you."

Gerald flopped around like a fish until he came to a sitting position, legs out straight in front of him. John wasted no time in tying him up, pulling a cloth gag from his back pocket and tying it tight around his mouth. He tapped the surface of the fake watch, laughing before shoving him down flat on the floor.

"Don't move, and don't make a sound. If you do, I will shoot you."

"Mffffff." Gerald tried to talk, but his voice was meek, muted. John rolled his eyes.

"You can talk when we get there. Might want to think about what you're going to say, though, because I am not in the mood for anymore of your shit." He kicked him in the leg for the hell of it, pulling himself into the front of the van and starting the engine. As soon as he was off the block, he pressed the relevant buttons on his phone to switch the area of the kill feeds. Checking his own Rolex, he was pleased to see he was right on time. He just hoped that the most important part of the plan worked out. He didn't have another option. It was do or die.

The streets were light on traffic, with no sign of a police car or anything amiss. The cameras being down would have triggered a bit of panic, but the feed wasn't down long enough for any major investigation. He'd used the tech many times, on smaller scales, but this wasn't some bustling metropolis. Andersen Falls was a place that boasted a low crime rate.

Until he'd arrived, of course. But all of that was down to the whimpering man in the back. He had underestimated his foe, for once. It didn't sit well with him.

Just on the outskirts of town, he hung a left and drove down the track he'd driven down a few times since his arrival here. The loose gravel crunched under his tires as he pulled to a stop outside the dilapidated building. He stepped out. There was no one around, the whole place silent but for the occasional squeak of the van as its occupant writhed around inside.

I should just kill him. Make him disappear. It was John's speciality, once upon a short time ago. It would solve a lot of problems. He could just go poof and then Bella and the kids would be free of him. No more legal wrangling. Bella wouldn't have to see the younger woman he'd cheated on her with draped over some fancy car in little more than a bikini whenever she passed a town billboard or saw a Day-Glo flyer on her car windshield.

If she lived that long. Gerald seemed determined to take out the mother of his children, and John wasn't about to let that happen.

The children were the point, though. John couldn't take the only father they had away from them, leaving them to wonder why he had walked away without a backward glance, never to contact them again. He knew what it was like to not have a family.

He wouldn't be able to take Gerald away from them, as pitiful as he was. Especially if he would have to be there for the fallout, for the pain that followed. He couldn't watch the four of them go through that, knowing it was his fault. He was already keeping so much from them.

He'd never felt so out of control. Out of his depth. For the first time in his life, he had something to lose, and he was ready to burn the fucking world down to the studs to keep it from happening. Taking risks was something he always managed, but tonight, he was going to take the biggest risk of his entire life.

He just hoped at the end of it, he still had what he wanted.

He wanted Bella and the kids, forever. He wanted to watch the kids grow up, and he wanted to take care of their mother like no one ever had. Give them all a better life. Make Bella see how absolutely stunning she is, every day. Follow her anywhere her career took her. He wanted to be the man of her dreams, the one she wrote all of her books about. He could see a life, a future–for the first time in forever–and tonight, he was going to keep her safe. Once and for all.

Entering the space he'd procured when he came to Andersen Falls, he looked around. Everything was in place, ready for him to finally end this. And hopefully, he could keep what he couldn't live without.

———

Gerald spluttered and coughed, water dripping down his nose as he shook his head like a wet dog.

"Hey!" he shouted. "Let me go!"

John answered by throwing another bucket of ice water over him, his face passive as Gerald gasped and shuddered.

"Stop!" He opened his eyes, taking in the fact he was in the middle of a huge gray storage area. He flexed his arms against the leg and arm restraints tying him to the chair, grunting like a stuck pig when he realized he wasn't getting out of this. "Help! Help!"

John stepped forward, the sound of his palm slamming across his cheek echoing through the room. "Shut up. I am doing the talking now. No one will hear you here. No one knows where you are, Gerry. Your phone has been disposed of, there isn't a camera in Andersen Falls that saw you leave the car lot. In fact, if I had the choice, no one would see or hear from you ever again. Not even a piece of you would be found, and it's what you deserve."

The gag now hanging loose around his neck, Gerald was keen to argue his case. "You can't do this. You're crazy!"

"Oh, I'm not the crazy one here, my simpering little captive. You need to realize that your days of controlling people and pushing people around are done." He pulled the tripod into view, the red light of the camera blinking as he fixed the lens right on Gerald. Taking out the knife from his back pocket, he tapped the top of the camera with it. The light from the lamp he'd erected just so was enough to singe his retinas a bit and allow him to crank up the fear level. Hence the dingy, out of the way place, the restraints, and the camera.

He wanted Gerald to feel helpless. Just like Bella would have if one of the insane assholes he'd hired had succeeded in whatever warped plan they had. Some of those guys were not clean-cut killers. Some of them took their time to torture, too.

The thought of Bella at the hands of one of those sociopaths made John's fists tingle to punch Gerald in the face again. He set everything up instead, the purpose of the evening fuelling his control.

"It's time to tell the truth, Gerald. Your days of controlling your family are over."

And he hit the record button.

Once it was done, he sent a message to Bella, dropped a pin at his location, and waited. Heart in his throat, after what seemed like forever, he finally heard the door open.

"John?" she called out, and he came out of the shadows.

Bella screamed the second she saw him. John's heart had never beat so fast. He felt sick, seeing that look of fear on her face. Fear of *him*.

He grabbed her before she got near the door.

CHAPTER
TWENTY
BELLA

"Help!" The man was hulking, his balaclava-covered face terrifying as he lunged for her. "Let me go!"

"It's me. It's okay."

That voice. It couldn't be. He wouldn't do this, right? When she'd got the call from him asking him to meet her here, she'd been weirded out enough when she saw the place. She should have followed her instincts and drove back home. Instead, she risked dying in a warehouse at the hands of a man she'd fallen for.

A man who, apparently, didn't exist.

As she struggled in his too familiar, muscular arms, she idly wondered who would play her in the TV movie. Maybe Constance could sell the rights and help look after her kids once she was found chopped into little bitty pieces.

"Listen, I am not going to hurt you. I'll let you go, but you can't leave." His words were comforting. Or they would have been, if she still trusted him. And if he didn't have his gloved hand over her mouth. "Nod if you understand me. This is not what you think. Ready? Nod if you understand."

She bit down on his finger, but he didn't even flinch. The hand around her waist just gripped her tighter. "That's my feisty girl." His hand dropped from her face, and she tried to headbutt him. He dodged it, chuckling as he picked her up into his arms. "Now, I have something to show you, and as much as I like fighting with you, it's not what you're here for." He sat her in a metal chair in the centre of the room and stepped to the side.

"G…Gerald?"

Gerald's scream was garbled, cut off by the rag taped to his mouth. His eyes were wide as he struggled against his bindings. His shirt was spotted with blood, his left eye swollen, already purpling.

John tore off his balaclava, tucking it into the back pocket of his jeans.

"John?" she whispered, her voice croaking. "What are you doing? What is this?"

His smile was rueful, his expression soft. It didn't fit the horror show she was witnessing.

"I'm protecting you, Bella. I have been since the minute we met."

Shrinking back in her chair, her eyes flicked to the door. She could make it, get help. If she could make it to the car…

"You won't make it to the parking lot," he said softly, holding the keys he must have grabbed from her in their scuffle. "I will never hurt you. Or the kids. I know you don't trust me, but it's the truth." He swallowed. "I love you. All this is for you."

Gerald made a noise. It almost sounded like a laugh.

John kicked the swivel chair he was strapped to, spinning him a few yards away without taking his eyes from hers. "Gerald hired someone to kill you." His jaw flexed. "Me."

"W-what?" *I'm dead. He killed me the second I walked in. Or I hit my head or something. Make it make sense.*

"I'm not a consultant, which I guess you already figured out. My name is John Smith now, but I've had many names. Killed many people. Bad ones. People who ruin countries and murder good people. I did it for years. Traveling. Being anonymous."

Gerald screamed again, jiggling in his chair as he tried to get away.

John levelled him with a look that froze him on the spot. "Gerald, one more noise and you know what happens."

Bella put her head in her hands, but she didn't even feel it. She felt…numb. Like her arms didn't belong to her body. "You kill people."

"Killed. Past tense." He grimaced. "Well, I did kill recently, but he was a scum of the earth hitman Gerald hired to murder you once he knew I wasn't going to do it."

"Gerald did this." She turned to her ex, waiting for him to scream again, but the second she looked him in the eye, she knew. "You hired John to kill me?"

"Yes," John confirmed. "But I had no intention of taking the job. I didn't take his money. I came to town to protect you, to stop it from happening. He got impatient, and I warned him off. Didn't I, Gerald?" His voice was almost playful now, teasing. "I told you to shut it down, but you didn't listen. So, I had to kill the hitman." He raised his hands in the air as if he'd been caught with his hand in the cookie jar. "But I swear, he's the last one. I am retired. I was before I came to Andersen Falls. It was my last job. When I knew it was you at risk, I couldn't stay away. I got close, to protect you. To protect Evan, Daisy, and Poppy. And everything I told you regarding us is true. I fell for you, probably before I even knew you. I was going to make sure you were safe and then leave, but I couldn't. I just…I fell, Bella."

This is a fever dream, she told herself. *A concussion.* "How? Why?" She hadn't heard him approach, but suddenly he was kneeling before her. His hand reached out, but he placed it on his lap at the last second. "I don't understand any of this."

Gerald was still trying to speak, but she couldn't take her eyes off John. All the pieces of their relationship were flashing through her mind as she tried to reconcile what she knew with what he was telling her. What she could see with her own eyes.

"I know, Belle."

"Don't call me that."

The flash of pain that flashed across his face was hard to miss, but she didn't take it back. She felt so stupid, so utterly stupid. If she wrote this into a book, she would have deleted herself. Deemed the heroine of the story as being two-dimensional and dumb. "My readers would never buy this," she mumbled to herself, her thoughts reaching her voice box before she could stop them. Gerald screamed again, and the muffled cry broke her out of her stupor. She was on her feet and in front of him before she even registered the movement.

"Mmffff!" His eyes were wide, pleading.

She looked back at John as her hands reached for the gag, but he just nodded and sat down heavily in the chair she'd vacated. She ripped off the tape, taking some of his skin and the rag with it.

"Argggh!" he complained. "Careful, B!"

"Careful! You hired someone to kill me!"

"No, no! I didn't, I–"

"Stop lying," John cut in. "I have the tape, remember?"

"Tape?"

John pointed to a tripod in the corner, a camera mounted on top. "Yep. That's what we've been doing this afternoon, right, Gerry boy? A nice, incriminating home movie. And I have more evidence, too. The PI he hired to photograph your house, for example."

"You hired a PI?"

Gerry was a stammering mess, blood from his torn lip dripping down his quivering chin.

"How could you do this? What about the kids?" He didn't answer, so she slapped him across the face with the back of her hand as hard as she could. "Answer me, Gerry! What did I do to you, huh? Except love you, raise our kids, and work my ass off! All while you played the big man around town, did the bare minimum with the kids, and then boinked your staff!"

"I didn't do any of that, he's lying! And you have no room to talk, you're sleeping with him!"

"Careful," John's voice was all growl. "Watch how you talk to her. I won't warn you again."

"Oh yeah? Well, bring it, GI Joe! You can't do a thing to me, can you? Not really. What are you going to do, kill the father of her kids? Hey!"

Gerry's head bounced off the concrete as his chair tipped backward from the force of Bella's kick. She didn't stop there. Grabbing him by the chest, she shook him again and again, pummelling her fists against his chest as she finally let her anger take the wheel over her fear and confusion. "You were going to kill their mother! Why, Gerry? Why?"

She was still shaking the hell out of him when she felt two strong hands pull her up.

"He's not worth it, Bella. He's not worth your energy." She felt his arms band around her, and she kicked Gerry in the leg, making him howl before John scooped her into his arms. "Please, calm down. You're going to hurt yourself." He sat her back in the chair, pulling away to kneel at her feet again.

Gerry was crying openly now, his snivelling moans echoing around the room. "Bella, we have to deal with this. People are going to start missing us eventually."

Bella realized she didn't know what time it was. The world was a completely different place than it had been before she'd walked through those doors. She didn't recognize her life anymore. "I have to get back, for Erin. She has plans with friends later. She's got the kids."

John nodded once, striding over and righting Gerry. "I'll untie him when you're gone, clean up here."

She nodded, her mind whirling.

"You go back to the house. Don't talk to anyone about this, Belle. I mean it. I can keep you safe, but you have to pretend it never happened."

Gerry, however, wasn't done. "Oh, I won't forget this happened." He spat blood at John's feet. "I won't forget this. Ever. I am going to sue you for full custody. I am not having him around my kids. You will sell the house immediately, and stop coming after me for alimony. There's no money, anyway. Daisy saw to that with her little Internet stunt. They'll need a parent, and Brittany wants kids. You can do what you want once I have them back. Marry the murdering bastard for all I care, but this goes my way now. You can't kill me, and you can't show that tape. No one will believe you, anyway. Who would? I can say I was worried about the man my wife was dating and–"

"Ex-wife," John snarled. "And what happens next isn't up to you. I can snuff you out without blinking, you little piss ant. The only reason I haven't is because I know Bella wouldn't want that." He got in Gerry's face, his easy smile draining the color right out of his captive's face. "Don't push me any further, or I might just forget my promise and end you."

John turned and trained his eyes on Bella. "What do you want to do? You don't need him or his money. I have more than enough, if you need it. I can take care of all of you. Forever."

"John, I can't talk about this."

His swallow was audible. "I know. I get it. I broke your trust, and I promised I wouldn't, but I had to do what I did to protect you. Once he'd ordered the hit, I knew what I had to do. I would never have hurt you. I came here to stop it. To stop anything and everything that was coming to hurt you, and I did. Happily."

"Yeah." Her voice cracked with a sob she kept back. "And you lied and schemed, just like him. I never knew you, not really."

"I don't agree. Bella, you are the one person in the world who truly knows me. I know it's a lot to take in, but I meant what I said. I love you. So much. Burn the world down love you. Whatever you decide, I'll make it happen. Even if it means turning myself in. Hell, if you asked me to kill him right now, I would. The important thing is that you and the kids are safe. I can live with anything else, as long as I know that."

"Touching," Gerald sneered from behind him. "The Belle of the ball and Dexter the fricking serial killer. Very Romeo and Juliet."

"One more word, and I'll blow your kneecaps off and feed them to you," John growled, not bothering to look his way. "Bella." The way he said her name, with such softness and affection, it broke something in her. "Tell me what you want."

———

Bella had only been home a couple of hours when the doorbell rang.

When she'd returned, shaken and hiding a bloodstained blouse under her coat, Erin had taken one look at her shell-shocked face and offered to change her plans and take the kids out for a movie and pizza. The kids, all loving Erin, had been thrilled and didn't even ask where John was in their excitement for junk food and an afternoon not stuck in the house. She'd given Erin a wad of cash and bundled them out the door, spending the next half hour in the shower crying. The washer helped to dispose of the evidence of her afternoon.

The bell rang again, and she steeled herself to face what was behind it. Prising herself off the couch, she pulled her bathrobe tight and reached for the wine she'd been nursing.

"Hi." He'd changed. Gone was the dark clothing and the black balaclava. John looked normal, standing there in midnight blue jeans and a white sweater. She kept her eyes below his collar. Looking him in the eye right now would probably take her off her feet. "Can I come in?"

She shrugged, turning to head back to the couch. "Sure. You've probably got a key, anyway, right? You updated my security system. You probably know more about this place than I do."

She heard his heavy sigh as she settled back down into the overstuffed cushions. The TV was muted, the news channel on the screen. She'd been watching it since she came home, half expecting John's face to pop up.

He took a seat in the chair opposite, his long legs stretched in front of him as he waited for her to look at him.

She could feel his eyes on her, like she always did when he was near. This was the first time that she didn't want it. Her mind was still scrambling, her brain scattered. And her heart? Well, that was broken. Bleeding from all the holes that had been shot through it in that warehouse. Gerry might as well have killed her, because she felt like part of her had died in there.

"Where are the kids?"

"Erin took them for the afternoon. I think I scared her, to be honest. I told her we'd had a fight." She chuckled, but it was empty, devoid of any humor. "Queen of the understatement, huh?"

"I'm sorry you're upset."

She shook her head, feeling the tears well up. "It's my turn to talk."

John fell silent.

She kept her eyes focused on anything but him. "You know, it's not the fact that my ex-husband hired someone to kill me. Well, it was a shock, of course. Actually, it's pretty terrifying, but I get it, in a weird way. Now that I know his finances, his behavior makes more sense now." Draining her glass, she leaned forward and refilled it from the open bottle of chardonnay on the table. "I watch a lot of true crime, you know. Netflix has a lot of documentaries on this sort of thing. Husbands finding a new life and not wanting their old one. Women just divorce their men, usually. I mean, there's the odd bumping off, but it's mostly the men who do it. The stats prove that. Wives demand things, for their kids, for the life they need to keep going when their spouse wants out. I called the bank after the kids left." Her free hand clenched in her lap. "He'd tried to remortgage our house a couple of months ago. They wouldn't let him, of course, not without my co-signing. I'd already told them we were in the process of a divorce when I called for a settlement figure for the solicitor. I think, looking back, that I figured he might do something sly. I mean, I had no intention of selling, but I was doing the right thing, you know? I've always done the right thing. Raised the kids, put up with the PTA, hit my deadlines. Or tried to. Family life got in the way at times, but I was pretty good at winging it."

The chardonnay hit the back of her throat as she took a big swig. She welcomed the slight numbness it brought, the tingle of her muscles as the wine helped uncoil them. "We were good in the first couple of years, but then we had Evan, and the first gym took off. We got busy, and I guess I just figured he was stressed." She shook her head as a single tear fell. "But the truth was, he was lazy. And he never really bothered about the whole family thing, not really. He was all about status and money. He wanted to be the big man around town, and he was, in a way."

As she brushed another tear away, John dropped a handkerchief onto her lap. It was white, pristine. She took it, playing with the hem for a moment before using it to wipe the tears from her cheek. She felt him sit on the couch, away from her, but close enough to smell his familiar scent.

"I knew he was hiding things, acting erratically," she continued. "He was dodging the divorce and the settlement. I just thought he didn't want to pay up. I know Brittany wants the finer things, the big life. They're both similar in that way. I just didn't think he'd want to murder me to get it. He was still on my life insurance, for God's sake." Another mouthful of wine. "He'd have come out of it pretty good. He hated what Daisy did to his reputation. Playing the grieving father would have been a real plot twist."

"I would never have let that happen."

"Yeah, and you killed someone. To protect me."

"Jennings was…like me, but different. He never followed the code I did."

"The code? Jesus," she huffed. "You really are Dexter."

"No, I'm not. I never got off on killing people."

"But you took the job to kill me."

"No! Bella, no. I took the job to protect you. I have never taken the life of an innocent person. Never."

"So, you knew all this, from the beginning."

"Yes. I came here for you."

"You came here for me."

"Yes, I came to Andersen Falls to protect you. I warned Gerry that you were not to be touched, and when he hired the PI, and then Jennings, I took care of it."

"You killed the PI, too?" Wine sloshed over the rim of her glass as she jerked forward in her seat. "Oh my God, I'm going to be sick." He reached for her, but she shrank from him. "Don't touch me."

"Sorry. I'm so fucking sorry, Bella. For a lot of it." *A lot of it.* She drained her glass and reached for the bottle, but he got there first, pulling it out of her reach. "No more drinking. It won't help."

"It fricking well might! You killed two people for me!"

"No." He was next to her now, his knees almost touching her thigh. His hands reached for her, but he didn't touch her. The irony was, if she let him hold her, under any other circumstance, she would have felt better. Safer. "Bella, the police dealt with the PI. I never touched him, and Jennings was evil. He needed to be dealt with. He would never have stopped coming for you. The second he got the deposit–"

"Deposit, from Gerry?" She sank back against the cushions. "He paid you, too, right?"

"Yes, but I didn't keep the money."

"Right," she laughed, but it came out as a choked sob. "That's all right, then."

"No, it's not, but I had no choice except to take the job. I would never have taken it on, but when I found out it was you, I had to come for you. To stop it. To protect you, and your kids. I did what I had to, Belle, because I love you. All of you. I never expected it, but I do."

"No, you just pretended to date me, to get around my kids. To be in their lives. Our lives."

"I never pretended. I knew you were on the dating app, and I saw it as a way to get close, yes, but I wanted to date you. For real. I told myself I would leave once you were safe, but I can't go. I don't want to. Not now. I'm in love with you. I have never been in love before you. I never thought I could. I didn't think I deserved it. I didn't have a life like other people. I bounced around in foster homes, and then on the street. I got recruited and trained. It was a life, one I believed in. Anything I did was to protect people from evil, from the horrible people who hurt other people. It wasn't all murder. I investigated people, just like the FBI would. We just had different resources, and our methods were a little further under the radar. I was getting out, Bella. I didn't come here as part of that. I had already left. I was done, but when Gerry did what he did, I accepted the job with no intention of seeing it through."

He loves me. He'd said it in the warehouse, but in the noise and the shock she hadn't even thought about it. What it meant. A few days ago, if he'd told her that, she would have been over the moon. Because she loved him, too. She'd come back to life with him around. He was the perfect man. Protective, good with the kids. Careful with her heart. He not only thought her career was more than a hobby, but he was in awe of her. Had read every book. Cheered her on. The hero in the book she was writing was him. Every bit of the character in her pages was John Smith. She brought him to life in her book, just as he had breathed new life into her by being there. By loving her. Casey Bainbridge, the hero in her story, was sitting right next to her, flesh and bone.

And neither of them was real.

"Your name isn't John Smith, is it? Daisy made a joke once about it being a good name for someone to have, to blend in. Her hacker senses are still there, obviously. It's just her mother who's stupid."

He hiccupped a sigh, and she thought she saw him wipe at his eyes before answering. "You're not stupid. It's the name I chose for my new life. It's the last name I will ever have."

"And what was your name before that?"

"At work, I was Mr. Black."

She huffed an incredulous laugh. "Very Usual Suspects. Do you even have a real name? One your parents gave you? You had parents, right? Or were you made in some Secret Service lab?"

The corner of his lips lifted, just for a second. "My parents–or my mother, I should say, because I don't know if my father was involved beyond my conception–left me in the street at a clinic in Brooklyn. I only had the clothes on my back and a blanket. Back then, they tried to trace where I came from, but no one got anywhere. I could probably find out, if I wanted to look."

"You didn't have a name?" She had a flash of delivering her children in the hospital, with Gerry by her side. She couldn't imagine what it took to leave a baby without even giving him a name before saying goodbye.

"I did, but a social worker named me. She was a big music fan."

"Let me guess," she quipped. For some unfathomable reason, she wanted to lighten the moment. "Hendrix. Elvis?"

He smiled, and she couldn't help but think how much she'd missed this, between them. Laughing and joking with each other, teasing that smile out of him. She looked away.

"Well, babies with no parents were called Smith in that area, and as I was never adopted officially, she named me after her idol, Johnny Cash."

"No. I don't believe you."

"Bella, I have never lied to you. Not on things that matter. Not directly. I have avoided the full details, but I have always tried to protect your trust with the truth. My birth name is Cash Smith. John is my middle name. I liked my social worker. She stuck with me over the years. I wasn't the easiest kid. I was pretty angry from a young age, but she always looked out for me. She died a few years ago, but I always said to myself that when I got out, I would take that name back. In honor of the only person who gave a shit enough to care, to give me a name."

"So, your name really is John Smith?"

There was that smile again. Her heart leaped, betraying her. "Yes. I dropped the Cash bit. Too memorable."

And there it was, a reminder of the truth. "Because you still need to keep a low profile."

He shrugged. "I'm out, free and clear. I just got used to blending in." He sucked in a deep breath and ran his hand through his hair. "I dealt with Gerry."

Gerry. She hadn't even thought about him. "Do I even want to know?"

"I took him to see a friend of mine. Got him patched up. He's not going to talk. It's over. No one else is coming after you."

"Thank you, I guess. I still have to deal with the debt."

She looked around her house, the pictures on the windowsill of the kids. Poppy's drawing on the side table. "We'll have to sell the house. I've had a bump in book sales recently, so cash flow is good for the moment, but when the business fraud comes out, it will be messy."

"No, it won't. He signed the papers. The house belongs to you now."

"How?" John's look turned sheepish. "Oh. You fixed it, right? Did you pay him off?"

"I took care of you and the kids."

"That's not an answer, John."

"I dealt with it. The agency owed me a favor after sending Jennings here. Let's just say, my old boss knows he messed up. It's done. Gerry's going to sell up and liquidate his assets to get back into the black."

Nodding, she couldn't help but think of her children. "I don't want him around here. Ever again."

"He won't be. It will hurt the kids, him leaving, but–"

"I don't care. He never deserved them. I won't have them near him. I think I'd kill him myself if he tried to be a father now." She bit at her lip. "I guess we'll have to see if he gets in touch."

But she knew he wouldn't. He'd never been that invested. They were just a tool in all this. With her gone, he'd have palmed them off on anyone and everyone. They would never have been a priority. Her eyes fell to the clock on the wall. "They'll be back soon. You should go."

She picked up the empty wine glass, but his hand wrapped around hers as she rose to her feet.

"I am sorry, Bella. I know I scared you in the warehouse. I just couldn't have anyone else coming after you."

"Are you really sorry?" His thumb stroked along her fingers, and she stared at it. Felt the rough skin against hers.

Working hands. She remembered thinking of him out there in the world, protecting countries with his security firm. Now, she had to add choking dictators and offing hired killers to the list. The body that had made her feel so safe had done things she'd never even thought of. "About everything?"

"I'm sorry I broke your trust. I can't be sorry for the things I did to protect people, or to protect you. I am not ashamed of who I am anymore than a soldier would be for what they do for their country. I'll say it again; I never killed an innocent person."

Looking into his eyes, she knew he was telling the truth. It might have been naïve, but she believed him. He was a good man. If it wasn't for him, Evan, Daisy, and Poppy would be without a mother. She would have been snuffed out, and Gerry would have gotten away with everything he'd plotted.

"I understand."

His smile made her heart clench. "You do? Oh, Bella, I'm so relieved. I know it will take time, but–"

"You should go, John." She pulled her hand out of his grasp. "They'll be back soon, and you can't be here when they get here."

His face crumpled. "I know what you're doing. Please don't."

"I have to." She stood up, her trembling legs barely able to hold her up. "I can't do this. I don't trust you anymore."

"I'll earn it back. I would never hurt you. Any of you. I love you. Don't do this, baby."

She leaned against the door frame for support. "It would never work. Not after everything. Not after the way we started. The kids are going to need me, with Gerry gone. They've been through too much already. And what if someone comes for you?"

"They won't. I'm out. For good. No one's coming." When he moved closer to her, she stepped into the hallway, away from him. He froze, a devastated look marring his features. "You're scared of me?"

"No," she started to say. She meant it, too. It wasn't him that scared her; it was everything that had happened. How dangerous it had been. A life with him seemed impossible. She should have followed her gut and stuck to research only. Falling in love with John Smith had opened up her world, but she didn't trust her own judgement right now. The man she had raised a family with had hired her boyfriend to murder her. She needed a minute to let the truth fully sink in.

"You are. You can't wait to get away from me." He looked down at his hands. "I get it. I never wanted to tell you. I knew this could happen."

"John, the kids are coming. I can't deal with this, not right now."

"Do you love me?"

Her heart hammered in her chest. Despite her adult, rational brain telling her otherwise, all she wanted to do was tell him her truth. Make it work, somehow. Throw caution to the wind and lean into the life he'd shown her. He was retired, so it wasn't like she'd be washing his butcher knives along with the dishes in the evening or taking bloodstained shirts to the dry cleaners. He'd saved her life. Had been there for her and the kids. Had loved her with a fierceness she'd never known before, and never would again.

But she couldn't say it. Couldn't reconcile what she knew with what she felt. She still saw that man in the warehouse, making Gerry scream. They were from different worlds. After all this, her kids had been through enough, and she needed to focus on the aftermath. Get life back to normal. Do the right thing. She always did the right thing.

He stepped closer, his eyes on hers like he was waiting for her to run. Which was right on the money.

"Belle, I'm in love with you. If you don't feel the same, I promise I will leave. And I'll never bother you again. Just tell me." He was so close now, she could see the flecks of gold in his eyes and the stubble on his chin. "Baby, do you love me back?"

Time stopped as she looked into his hopeful eyes. She memorized the details. The tiny scar he had above his left eyebrow. The way his short hair changed color in the light that streamed in through the hallway window. She knew every inch of him, understood the man he was. So much was a question mark, but everything he'd been through had made him the man standing in front of her. She could never hate him.

A car door outside broke the silence. Poppy's happy little laugh from the driveway broke the moment, and she tore her gaze away.

John's breath puffed out in a sigh. "I'll go out the back door." When she turned to him, he wore a dejected expression. "Look after yourself, Bella. I will always love you."

He flashed her one of his brightest smiles, and then he was gone.

The pain was a slug to her chest. She never said it. She'd let him leave thinking she wasn't in this with him. She had to tell him. She had to go after him…

"Hi, Mom!" Poppy burst through the door like a bull at a rodeo. "The movie was so funny! There was this magic crayon, and it was purple!"

"Oh, wow!" She plastered a smile on her face as Evan, Daisy, and Erin came through behind her. "Sounds amazing, Pops! You two enjoy it, too?"

Daisy shrugged, and Evan asked what was for dinner.

Erin rolled her eyes. "We had fun, and Evan ate a whole pizza by himself, so there's no rush on dinner." Her smile faltered. "You get everything sorted?"

Nope. Not even a little bit. My heart just left out the back. "Yes, I think so."

She bent down to drop a kiss against Poppy's head. "Now, tell me more about this crayon."

CHAPTER
TWENTY-ONE
JOHN

Six Months Later

Code Name: Mr. Black
Status: Retired
Whereabouts: Unknown
Last mission: Completed, details redacted

The window display stopped him in his tracks. Almost dropping his keys down the grate, he snatched them off the sidewalk and fought the urge to press his nose to the glass.

Baltimore author, Bella Carmichael – get your copy here!

The whole display depicted copies of her book, but he barely took them in. He couldn't tear his eyes off her. She looked different from her past author photos. Her hair was shorter, the honey highlights showcasing her beautiful face.

God. I miss her.

Setting up his new business in the unit next door to the book shop he'd invested in wasn't the best idea, he realized now. The stock of her books had been selling well, so well that the town of Hamilton had obviously fallen in love with her. He couldn't blame them. It's not like he'd moved far. He could emigrate to the end of the earth and she'd still be there. She was in his head, and his heart.

"Don't buy it," he told himself. "You've been good. Don't break your streak."

He had been good. It had been a good few weeks since he'd checked on her. He'd made a point of not checking her emails, had ditched the cloning of her phone. He'd pulled his private security detail after the first three months, once he knew for sure the threat was gone. Gerry had dropped out of his family's life the second the ink dried on his exit papers. He was alone, because once Brittany realized he was out of money after setting things right, she left him. The last John had seen of her, she was on his TV screen on a dating reality show. It seemed Gerry had lost on all counts, but he also hadn't tried to contact his children, or Bella.

Which was a good thing, because it meant that John didn't have to break his promise to her and kill again.

The stacks of books looked good, and John's eyes devoured the cover. It looked different from her previous ones. Then, he noticed a detail that made his heart stop.

He pushed the door open, and went to see his favourite bookshop owner.

Twenty minutes later, sitting at his desk next door, he sank back into the supple leather of his chair. Prince Securities was thriving, and he was getting more and more contracts all the time. Some of his old security consultant buddies were working for him now, and they did the overseas contracts. Protection detail only, of course. So far, he'd overseen the security for several diplomats, high profile clients, and even a country singer that Bella would have squealed to hear about.

She was a big fan, and when John met the singer's team about the contract, all he'd wished for was being able to tell her about it.

It was a far lonelier existence he led now, and he hated it. He'd never been bothered before. Sure, it had been a solitary life, but he was busy and his work was important. He figured not ever having a family primed him for such a life, but now, when he went back to his apartment, filled with furniture Bella had helped him pick out, he longed for the chaos and the clutter of her house.

He missed the kids. The football games, the pizza nights. Talking about coding with Daisy, whom he was pretty sure would be running the country behind the scenes one day. He missed Poppy's sense of style, her confidence in who she was, and her ability to just be happy. Most of all, he missed their mother. The way she made him feel. Watching her laugh with her children and the way she was there for them. He missed her touch, her scent. The way her eyes sparkled when she looked at him. Her grumpy, pre-coffee, gremlin self in the morning. The cute little way she stuck her tongue out when she was writing, tapping the keys and smiling when a plot point came together. She was electric, and he'd been well and truly shocked by her.

The phone on his desk rang, but he ignored it. He wasn't in the mood to work now. He couldn't think of anything but the parcel wrapped in brown paper on his desk.

Pulling the book out of its packaging, his finger ran along the embossed letters of her name, and then the little graphic. It was of a gun, the silencer attached to the gray steel drawing.

Protect My Heart, the title, was in red, standing out from the rest of the more muted colors. He turned it over, reading the blurb. His heart leapt.

It was about him, about them. Casey, the hero of the story, was a protective secret agent, charged with the task of saving a novelist from death threats made by a stalking superfan. She'd written their story, in a way, and he loved her for it. Perhaps, it was a way for her to work through things. He glanced at the reviews printed across the bottom of the cover.

Sexy, dangerous…addictive. – New York Times

Bella is back, with bite. – The Literary Review

He shouldn't have bought it. He didn't even know about the book since he'd blocked all news related to her from his Internet settings to stop himself from looking. Amazon had been a no-go, and he'd avoided reading new books altogether. Today had been the first time he'd bought a book from the shop next door. He'd spoken to the owner plenty of times, but only in the diner across the street or when they crossed paths at their front doors. Instead, he'd re-read the Bella Carmicheal books he already had as a way to feel close to her, seen through the new lens of knowing her so intimately. He'd felt irrationally jealous of the men she created in those stories, and now he was the hero of one.

But he didn't have her. He didn't get the girl, and he had to live with that. He was back where he had been for years. Alone, reading her books, and not having her in his life.

The phone rang again, and he picked it up with a gruff greeting. Roman spoke. "Hey, boss. Listen. We might have a problem on the job. I think we need another guy out here."

Roman was in the UK, part of the country singer's entourage.

"What's the problem, exactly? Is it the schedule?"

"The agent making the schedule is. He has her doing everything out here, and it's not exactly easy to scope out the places needed and protect her at the same time. We've had another letter threat, and I don't like how it's escalating. I could call Ryan, since he's finishing up the Germany thing, but I wanted to clear it with you first."

John stared at the book cover, his mind whirring. He could send Ryan. He only employed the best, and he would be happy to send in any member of his team. "No, don't ask Ryan. I'll do it."

Roman didn't say anything for a minute. "You, boss? I thought you were strictly wheels down."

John's eyes zeroed in on the book in front of him. He could stay around, in case she changed her mind. In case she needed him. He could stay on his own, working and living his new life. Wishing for some kind of signal that she wanted him again. But he wasn't stupid. She'd moved on, and he had to live with that.

"I was, but I think a change of scenery might be needed. I'll make the arrangements, and let you know when I land."

"Okay, boss. See you soon."

"Yeah. Any issues, let me know."

"Will do."

He ended the call and fired up the computer. It looked like he had a flight to book and a plane to catch. His hand caressed the letters of her name as he got to work. At least she'd be with him in spirit. He'd take the book with him, just like old times. Whatever way he could have Bella with him, he'd take it.

CHAPTER
TWENTY-TWO
BELLA

Bella heard the familiar shuffle of the kids on the stairs, and their whispering voices. Sundays were usually when she had a chance to sleep in, being the only day that none of them had school or extracurriculars to get to. The clock told her it was just after nine, but she'd been awake for hours. Had watched the sun rise through the raised blinds, wondering if she'd ever sleep properly again.

Her new book had taken off in a big way. It had only been out a few days, and already people were saying it was her best yet. Constance was absolutely thrilled, but Bella couldn't bring herself to be happy about it. It just reminded her of the man it was based on, and how he had gone from her life.

The first month, after the day she failed to tell John she loved him, had been hard. Harder than the divorce, and the scandal.

Gerry had done everything John told her he would. She received the deed to the house with her divorce paperwork, and the mortgage had been paid in full. Gerry's businesses had all closed down, and he and Brittany had split up. She was doing quite well now, having found a TV role on a reality show. She'd even been in touch with the kids, to say good-bye, which was more than Gerry did.

The kids had taken it surprisingly well. Poppy didn't even ask about him anymore, and the elder two seemed happier at not having to go see him. It made her sad, but it was far better than the alternative. They'd been more upset when she'd told them about her and John breaking up. Evan, in particular, had taken it hard. Poppy cried a lot, and Daisy…well, Daisy was Daisy. She kept her cards pretty close to her chest.

Those first few weeks, Bella had been there for them, and it was about the only thing holding her together. Then, she'd sat at her laptop, and the words had flowed out of her. She'd changed the book she was writing in favor of another story. About a writer in danger, and the elusive man who'd swooped in to protect her. She sat in Café Eleven every day while the kids were at school, pouring her heart onto the page. Looking up every time the bell on the door jangled, in case it was John.

Then, she'd gone to his flat and found it vacant. The phone number she had for him was no longer in service. By the time she'd realized that she still wanted him and had worked through the events through her writing, he'd done just what he'd said he would do.

He'd left her life.

She had no way to contact him. No way of looking for him. John Smith had left just as quickly as he'd come, leaving no trace behind. His landlord had no forwarding address. He was just…gone. Out in the world somewhere, thinking that she didn't want him anymore.

When the book came out, she'd been waiting by the phone. Hoping he'd read it, and that he would come for her. Get in touch, send a smoke signal, something. But as the days went by, her hope waned, and here she was, lying in bed wishing she'd just told him her truth. He'd come clean with his, and she hadn't been brave enough to do the same.

So, here she was. A few months ago, she would have been happy with how life had turned out. She was secure financially and safe, with Gerry as nothing but a bad memory. Her career had been rebooted, and a new contract had been secured with an eye-watering advance. She and the kids were set up for life, but it felt pointless. Empty. All of her previous problems had been resolved, but it wasn't enough. Not nearly enough anymore, because there was a John-sized hole in their lives.

"Do you think she's up yet?" Poppy, who was useless at whispering, was right outside the door.

Evan's deep voice sounded even deeper after his little sister's high-pitched tone. "Dunno. Maybe we should just leave her a bit. She's been working a lot."

"We could make her coffee. She might be less grumpy with coffee."

"Yeah, true. Daisy, is the coffee machine on?"

"Forget the coffee! We need to wake her up, now. We don't have time for this!"

Bella was just pulling back the covers as all three kids burst into the room. "What's going on?" She sniffed the air. "Haven't tried to make breakfast, have you? I still can't get the burn mark off the cabinet door from last time."

Poppy flounced onto the bed. "No. And I didn't mean to. I was only making pancakes."

"Yeah," Evan laughed, his hair stuck up at odd angles. "But they were gross. Who puts Skittles in a pancake?"

"Mickey Mouse did it on Clubhouse!" Poppy roared, charging at Evan. Daisy blocked her, handing her to Evan, who scooped her up and carried her out of the bedroom. "You suck, Evan!"

"Yeah, yeah. We need to get dressed."

"What is going on?" Bella asked as Daisy waggled a tablet in front of her.

"We need to go to the airport now."

"What?" So much for thinking her kids were doing well. They'd all lost their marbles. "What are you talking about?"

"John!" Daisy shouted. "He's leaving. Today."

The air rushed out of Bella's lungs, and she sank down onto the edge of the bed. "How do you know that?"

Daisy threw her a shifty look. "I saw his passport when we went to his place. I, er, made a note."

"Daisy, you didn't!"

Daisy shoved the tablet in front of her. "Yeah, well, sue me! I wanted to check him out, you know? After Dad."

Shit. Daisy was going to be the death of her. "And what did you find out?"

"Nothing, obviously, but I kept a track on him. He booked a flight, Mom. To London. One way. He's going to leave."

A bang came from Poppy's room. Evan laughed, and Poppy growled. "I am not a squirt, Evan! Take that back!"

"Get dressed in three minutes, and I will."

Daisy rolled her eyes, grabbing Bella by the arm. "Ignore them, Mom. Didn't you hear me? John's leaving. He might not come back! We have to stop him!"

Bella took the tablet from Daisy, who began flinging clothes out of her wardrobe at her. She was right. It was there. John had booked a flight to London, with no return. He really was leaving. The airport was their local one, which meant he hadn't gone far.

He'd stayed close, she realized, her heart pounding.

But by tonight, he wouldn't be. He'd be in England, and then she'd never see him again. He might change his name and never come back.

Daisy shoved a sweater over her head. "Mom! We need to go! Evan, are you ready?" She grabbed a pair of jeans from the bed and started thrusting one of Bella's legs through them. "Mom! Are you malfunctioning? Come on, we need to go! We want John back!"

That broke the spell. Evan and Poppy came running back in, fully dressed. Daisy shoved the other pant leg over her knee, jostling her to pull them up. "Wait. Just give me a minute." Daisy looked up at her, her determined face scrunched up tight. "You've been tracking him?"

"Well, I tried to. He pretty much went off the grid, until I got the ping this morning."

"Ping?" Daisy rolled her eyes. "Yeah, Mom. Ping. He booked the ticket and it triggered my tracker."

"Tracker?"

Daisy moaned, pulling her to her feet so fast she nearly fell over. With her half-dressed legs wobbling, she pulled them up the rest of the way. "Mom, I don't have time to talk about this. You barely understand Facebook."

Poppy chimed in, now fully dressed in a Transformer T-shirt and blue sweatpants. Her hat was backward on her head as per usual, shoved over her messy hair. "We love John, Mom. Can we go get him?"

"You love him?"

"Yeah," Evan said, a smile on his handsome face. "And so do you. No offence, but you've been miserable since he went. We know you broke up because of Dad."

Her hammering head stuttered to a stop. "Dad?"

"Yeah, because he was stressing you out and stuff. John left, and then Dad went. We're not stupid, you know. We know Dad doesn't do the right thing, but John made you happy. So, we've been talking, and we want John to come back."

She looked at each of her children, all dressed and ready for action. Their expectant faces were all waiting for her to move. "You've all talked about this?"

"Yeah," they said in unison. "We want to go get him, Mom," Evan said. "He comes to all my games, and he makes you happy."

"He stuck up for Poppy at school, too. And you. The kids don't hassle her anymore, and he knows all about coding," Daisy added.

"Yeah," Poppy giggled. "He dressed like a girl. It was so funny!"

"And you love him. We all do." Evan turned to the wardrobe, pulling her sneakers off the shelf. "You wrote a book about him, and you only did that for Dad before."

"We saw what you wrote," Daisy added. "In the front of the book." She lifted the tablet, showing the flight information on the screen. She pointed at the departure time. "I Google mapped the directions. We can make it!"

Evan picked Poppy up, heading for the door. "Come on, then, Carmichaels! What are we waiting for?"

As they headed to the stairs, Bella looked down at herself. The jeans and sweater her daughter had dressed her in over her PJs weren't the best, but they'd have to do. Smiling at Daisy, she grabbed the sneakers and shoved them onto her feet.

Daisy whooped, throwing her arms around her mother before running toward the stairs after her siblings. "She's coming, Evan! Grab the keys!"

"Woo hoo!" Poppy squealed. "This is the best day ever!"

———

The car journey to the Baltimore airport alone was enough to frazzle Bella's nerves. Evan had sat in the passenger seat, moaning about the traffic and messing with the satellite navigation to try to find a faster route. Poppy had insisted on listening to the Disney soundtrack and singing along to all the songs, much to the annoyance of everyone else in the car. Bella had driven as fast as she could without getting pulled over by the police or inciting a road rage nightmare, all while talking Daisy out of hacking the flight information and stopping the flight from taking off. After this was over, she was definitely going to start limiting screen time more. And Disney songs, for that matter. If she had to listen to *Let It Go* one more time, she was going to lose her mind.

They squealed into the car park, barely bothering to lock the car before breaking into a run. Evan hoisted Poppy onto his shoulders, and they sprinted across the car park, weaving in and out of the crowds of people pulling suitcases.

The automatic doors swiped open, and Daisy grabbed Bella's arm. "Over here, the departures board. It's not boarding time yet!"

They came to a screeching halt in front of the large electronic board. "Oh God, if he's checked in, though, they won't let us through without a ticket! I left my purse in the car!"

"There it is, Mom!" Poppy's chubby little finger pointed to the London flight listing. "What does gate mean?"

"It's where you board the plane, Pops. When they are ready, they put the number up." It wasn't there, so there was still a chance. The only thing was, the place was packed, they hadn't brought their passports, and she'd not brought her ID or credit cards.

"It's not going to work," Bella said, her voice empty. "We'll never make it. Look at the queues." The airport was bustling, travellers milling around the place and standing in huge lines waiting to check their luggage. "How are we supposed to find him?"

When she looked at her kids, she saw the deflated looks on their faces. They were too late, and they knew it. The notification had come through too late.

"There has to be something. What about a Tannoy announcement?"

"Yeah!" Daisy grinned. "We could go to Customer Services!" The three of them whirled around toward the desk, but it was packed. By the time they got a turn, the gate would be up. Getting through security would be impossible.

"Oh, God." Daisy looked to her mother for inspiration. "What can we do, Mom?"

Bella wanted to wipe the looks of devastation from their faces, but she felt numb. She'd driven them all here, wanting some kind of happy ending, but John was leaving. Would he even want to see her in the first place? After all this, even if she got to stand in front of him, would he want them now, after everything?

Evan whispered something to Poppy, and the little girl started to cry.

"Daddy!" She wailed, her voice getting higher. "I want my daddy!"

Daisy looked at Evan, and a look passed between them. Bella saw them both smile, and then they were shouting, too. "Dad! Dad! Where are you?"

I've finally broken them, Bella thought. *They're traumatized from having a feckless mother. They've all collectively decided to have some kind of meltdown.*

"Kids," she hissed out of the corner of her mouth, as people started to stop and turn their heads in their direction. Poppy was screaming over and over for her dad, and she could see people shooting them sympathetic looks. A couple of them began to come their way. "What are you doing? People are looking!"

Daisy winked at her. "Well, you won't let me ground the flight, so this is the next best thing. "John Smith!" She shouted across the airport lounge. "We are looking for our dad, John Smith. He's booked on flight 453. Can anyone help us?"

Poppy, who had stopped crying to listen to her sister, started to grin, but she covered it with her mouth. "Dad! John Smith is my daddy, and I can't find him."

Evan bit his lips together, and Bella knew he was holding in a laugh.

"Dear God," she mouthed to him. "I've created monsters." But she was smiling. She turned toward the open café area, calling to the diners who sat there. "Sorry, every-one," she lied. "My children are a little upset. We got stuck in traffic, and we wanted to wave my husband off. Have you seen him? He's called John Smith, and–"

"I'm here," a deep voice that spoke to her very soul called out.

Whirling around, the four of them found themselves looking at John. He stood there, suitcase by his leg, holding her book. For a moment, no one said anything. The people around them melted out of existence as his dark eyes took them in. Raising his hand, he pulled out the bookmark from *Protecting Her Heart,* lifting it to the page where her dedica-tion was typed.

For C.J.S.

The man behind the words.

I'm sorry I never said it when I had the chance, but I'm saying it now.

I love you. Come home.

"Hi, kids," he said, his lips curling into a happy smile as

he walked toward them. He came to a stop in front of Bella. "I was just starting to read your book in the café, when I heard you all." His grin widened. He fixed his gaze on Daisy. "I take it you found me?" She nodded, waving her tablet. His low chuckle was music to Bella's heart. "Smart girl."

"I pretended to cry!" Poppy chimed in, incensed that she wasn't getting any credit for her Oscar performance.

"It was my idea," Evan added. "Come on," he nudged Daisy. "I promised Poppy a cookie." The three of them headed off toward the café, leaving Bella and John standing there alone.

"I have my hands full," Bella said, her voice so choked with emotion she couldn't get the words that she wanted to say out. "I think I might need a partner."

"Oh, is that right?" John rumbled back, pulling her closer. "I know someone who might be able to help you there." He closed the book, dropping it to the floor to wrap his arms around her. "I loved your dedication, by the way. Did you really mean it?"

"Of course I did. I tried to find you, but you'd left. I was so stupid that day. Everything was so scary, and–"

"You don't have to apologize for anything, Bella. I should have told you sooner, but being around you, I just got deeper and deeper, and I was scared to lose what we had. When I saw your book, I thought you'd moved on. I was sitting in the café, waiting for my gate, and I read the dedication." He nodded his head toward his suitcase. "Another few minutes, and I would have been gone."

"Are you going on a job in London?" The thought of him still going, now that she was here with him again, touching him, was unbearable.

"I was. A protection detail. I just rang one of my team. He's going instead."

"You're staying? Really?"

"I'm staying. The second I read it, I'd made up my mind to come and beg you to be with me."

"Beg?" She smirked. "Well, that sounds nice, but I think the kids have already adopted you. They dragged me out of bed this morning to come here and get you. I love you, John. We all do. Come home? I know we have a lot to sort out, but–"

"Yes," he cut her off. "You have me, Belle. The beauty to my beast. You're mine, you and the kids. I want nothing more than to have a life with you all."

"And that's enough? Just us? Won't you miss the action?"

He answered her with a kiss. She melted into him the second his lips brushed hers, opening his mouth when he demanded entrance. He kissed her like he'd been waiting his whole life to do it, and she loved every second of it. When he finally pulled away, he caressed her cheek with a callused hand. "You are all the action I need," he grinned, just before the kids barrelled into them like a trio of screaming banshees, almost taking Bella off her feet. John held her tight, his arms solid around her.

"Come on, I think we made enough of a scene for today."

"Where are we going?" Poppy asked, her face red with excitement as John reached up to carry her in his arms.

"Well," John grinned, pulling Bella into his side, "I didn't eat breakfast this morning. How about we go for pancakes?"

Poppy gasped, strangling him with her death hug. "Deal!" she squeaked, her face suddenly gravely serious. "But I want mine with Skittles."

EPILOGUE

"Tonight, we have a very special guest on Baltimore Today. Bestselling author of *Over My Dead Heart*, multiple award winner, mother of three, and now screenwriter of the biggest movie of 2027, *Protecting My Heart*...Bella Carmichael-Smith!"

The audience clapped and whooped as Gloria Honey, the presenter, turned to Bella with a warm smile. "Now, Bella, I have been a huge fan for so many years, but it's safe to say that Over My Dead Heart is my favorite book of yours. How does it feel, finally seeing Casey on the big screen? Since *Protecting My Heart,* this series has just exploded. Always a New York Times and Amazon bestseller, foreign rights being snapped up worldwide, and now movie theatres booked solid for weeks. It must be amazing."

Bella smiled, thinking of the ride the last few years had been. "It really has, and I still have to pinch myself, to be honest. It was an honor being able to adapt the book for the screen, and a real learning curve, too. I am so grateful to the fans that stuck with me all these years, and for the new lovers of the Heart books."

"Well, Casey is an amazing character. He's so soft and gentle. Sexy and dangerous." Gloria turned to the audience. "What do you say, ladies? A man with a licence to kill, but he's a real gent, too!"

The audience collectively swooned and cheered like they were watching a Magic Mike concert and Channing was wiggling his abs.

"And he reads, too! Lord, have mercy! What would you say the inspiration was for his character? I know that in the past you did speak about the father of your children being a muse, but these days, you keep things even closer to your chest. Is Mr. Smith our Casey, or is he just a product of your amazing imagination?"

Bella looked past Gloria, into the wings at the side of the studio. John's dark eyes were already focused on hers. An ear piece trailing down his neck was the only sign that he was working. To protect her. Since things had taken off, he'd become her personal bodyguard, and she loved it. He mouthed, *I love you, beautiful*, at her, and she grinned before turning back to Gloria, that familiar blush only he gave her now showing on her cheeks. "Well, Gloria, my husband is a pretty private person, but I can tell you…" She raised a brow at the audience. "He is a lover of books, and only too happy to help me with my research." Everyone laughed, a chorus of oohs and ahhs rippling across the room.

In her ear, in the tiny microphone receiver John had given her, she heard the huff of his laughter. "Happy to provide more tonight, baby."

She squirmed in her seat, suddenly keen to get this over with and go back to the home they now shared together. Once the gates closed behind them, it would be just them and the kids. Which was how they liked it. Prince Security was doing well, and her books were practically writing themselves these days. She was happy, fulfilled, and inspired.

Gloria was wrapping up, and Bella pulled herself out of her daydream to focus on what she was saying.

"Well, I know we have a lot of ladies who are very grateful to your husband for that. We can't wait to see what's next. It's been a pleasure, Bella." She turned to Camera Two. "Bella Carmichael-Smith, everybody. If you haven't seen the movie yet, get those tickets while you can!"

Once the cameras were off and the audience was heading home, John found her. "You did great," he beamed. "I still can't believe my wife is such a star."

"You can't?" She pretended to pout. "I thought you were my biggest fan."

"Oh, I am." He kissed her like they'd been apart for months. Which was how it always felt with him. Perfect. Meant to be. "Casey is my favorite character. So handsome, clever."

"Modest," she giggled. "Kids okay?"

They'd left them at home, with Evan in charge. Which meant that when they got home, it would be chaos.

"Yep. Poppy wants pizza for supper. I said we'd order it on the way home."

"Sucker," Bella teased. "That girl has you wrapped around her little finger."

He chuckled as he led her through the studio to the waiting car. "Yeah, well, she knows how to play me, what can I say? They're growing up so fast, Evan will be off to college before we know it. I want to make the most of it, before we know it they'll all be off living their own lives."

"True," Bella agreed with a pang. "So, what will be next for us, when the nest is empty?"

John whirled her around in the corridor, crowding her

against the wall with his firm body. He kissed her neck, making her shiver. "Well," he drawled, taking his sweet, sweet time. "Naked Saturdays for a start. Travel. Grandkids."

"Grandkids?"

"Yeah." John beamed. "I can't wait to be a grandpa, when the time comes. We can show them the White House when Daisy finally exerts her power and takes over the world." They dissolved into laughter, his fingers finding hers and lacing them together. "I don't care what we do, as long as it's with you."

A muffled voice came through his earpiece, and he led her toward the door.

"All clear in the car park. Let's go home, Beauty. Once the kids are asleep, I have plans for you in the library." He fixed her with those dark, stormy eyes and she blushed at the thought of the night ahead. Naked Thursdays were definitely going to be fun.

"Lead the way, Beast," she told him, pulling him in for another kiss. "Take me home, baby."

MORE ROMANCE READS
FROM HARBOR LANE BOOKS

SWEET CHAOS
KIMBERLY QUINN

GIN GRIFFITH
DEMONS DON'T DO LOVE.
HOLY SMOKE
HELLBOUND BOOK ONE

GIN GRIFFITH
TEMPTATION HAS TEETH
CAT FIGHT
HELLBOUND BOOK TWO

C.A. KENNEDY
THE 7 HABITS OF HIGHLY EFFECTIVE REAPERS
THE GRIM REAPER CHRONICLES
BOOK ONE

ACKNOWLEDGMENTS

This book is different from anything I have ever written before, and for a long time the idea sat on my computer. When Harbor Lane Books read the synopsis, they saw something within it. What the book was about, and why my morally gray hero's story deserved to be told. They ran with it, and I will forever be grateful to Erica, Michelle, and all at Harbor Lane for their conviction in The Hitman's Love Contract.

I am so proud of the final book, and having written it through the added distractions of raising a family, having surgery, COVID, and even a broken leg, it's safe to say that seeing it out there in the world makes me feel like a proud new mother.

As ever, my first thanks goes to my publishing team, and to Tantor Audio.

The second round goes to my writer friends, who talked me down off the metaphorical ledge several times when I was in the muddy middle and felt the words THE END would never come.

Huge thanks to my husband, sons, and extended family. Thanks for putting up with me holing myself up in my little writing cave, and for all your help and support in my post-surgery recovery and when I was laid up after yet another bout of COVID, and while my broken leg healed.

Note to my readers – when you are cleaning your house to work through a plot point in your head, try not to carry too many dishes down the stairs. They bounced, but I didn't. Ouch.

Last but not least, thank you to my readers. Many have been with me for over a decade now, and I love to hear your thoughts on each and every book. Thank you for supporting me by buying the books, sharing the love online, borrowing from libraries, and for being so amazing in general.

I hope you love John as much as I do.

Until next time, happy reading!

ABOUT THE AUTHOR

I am a writer and teacher, living in West Yorkshire with my husband, our two sons, and our furry pets.

In July 2015, I won the Prima magazine and Mills & Boon Flirty Fiction Competition, with my entry, The Chic Boutique on Baker Street, out now in ebook and paperback.

The Flower Shop on Foxley Street followed this in 2017 and both books hit the Amazon top 200. I am the winner of the Writers Bureau Writer of the Year Award in 2016 and I have had work published in the UK and overseas in various magazines and newspaper publications.

I haven't stopped writing since, and I love every minute! I love to write romantic fiction, both rom-com and harder hitting women's fiction.

I am also a qualified post 16 teacher and have an MA in Creative Writing at Teesside University. I am a passionate autism awareness advocate and support families wherever I can. My eldest son, Jayden Dove published his own picture book for children in 2020, called Autistic Alfie, which is used in schools and libraries across the UK and is based on his own experiences.

In my spare time I love reading, crafts and travel. If you have enjoyed any of my books, I love to hear from readers on my socials! Just search for @writerdove and say hello, or show me your book photos!

ABOUT THE PUBLISHER

Harbor Lane Books, LLC is a US-based independent digital publisher of commercial fiction, non-fiction, and poetry.

Connect with Harbor Lane Books on their website www.harborlanebooks.com and on social media @harborlanebooks.

facebook.com/harborlanebooks

x.com/harborlanebooks

instagram.com/harborlanebooks

threads.com/harborlanebooks

pinterest.com/harborlanebooks

tiktok.com/@harborlanebooks

bsky.app/profile/harborlanebooks.bsky.social